HOBART

a literary journal

hobart.

Editor: Aaron Burch
Associate Editor: Mike McGowan

Hobart would like to thank many people. You are likely one of those. Thank you.

www.hobartpulp.com

Hobart is published bi-annually. In theory. For submission guidelines, please see the website, www.hobartpulp.com. Submissions are read year round and should be sent to submit@hobartpulp.com. Any other questions or comments can be sent to info@hobartpulp.com.

A portion of Pia Ehrhardt's "Chance" was previously published in *Pindeldyboz*. A very wonderful journal if we may say so ourselves.

All stories have been proofread and edited by the Hobart staff. Take that for what it's worth. We apologize. They deserved better.

Cover painting and all artwork by Andrew Feuk.

ISSN1544-788X
ISBN 0-9749541-0-1

Printed in Canada

Contents

John Leary
Daddy 8

Lee Klein
Brave Men Run 22

Susan Townsend
Family Therapy 34

Damon Stewart
Lost in the Static 42

Dennis Dillingham
Two Octogenarians Sitting at a Starbucks Drinking Orange Juice 60

Pasha Malla
Three Penises of Adelaide, South Australia 66

Shauna McKenna
Chance 76

Elizabeth Ellen
The Girl at the End of the Bar 86

Pia Ehrhardt
Hail 96

Max Ruback
Introduction to Still Life 104

Andrew Bomback
20 Stories About My Dead Brother, Ollie 108

Letter From the Editor

The likes. From the time we started the website, we had the idea to put up a list of the stuff we like and the stuff we don't. A silly, ever expanding list, that from the initial thought process of site design we thought to call (dis)likes. We were so clever. At the time the site was being read by a very very small handful of people, primarily old roommates, and it was a way to make those laugh who lived a couple of states away instead of a couple of doors down. It was almost all inside jokes and laughs at our own expense. Then the site started to grow. We were getting more and more submissions, and the quality continued to surprise, and with every update we added more things to the page; stuff we liked, stuff we didn't. We liked buddyhead.com, Joe Dirt, and "pinky rings "worth 'bout fitty"" and didn't so much care for Creed, Alien Resurrection or "Alex Rodriguez and Jason Giambi (and any other athlete we deemed to have sold out. the Rangers! the Yankees!?). And now A-Rod is on the Yankees too, and he is still on the dislikes. Our silly little lists, often made up fifteen minutes before updating the site, after weeks of thinking of things and then forgetting them all, resulted in emails praising our humor and telling us it was nice we didn't take it that seriously to long, rambly letters calling us "stereotypical and judgmental… pervasively cynical, pretentious with feeble little attitudes." All along, the likes remained stupid, dorky, and largely self referential, but they made us laugh, so we kept at them.

With this issue, we had the idea that it might be fun to hand over the lists to the contributors themselves. We have always been big fans of all things supplemental — amusing bios, when the author has a note to say how they wrote the story, or the genesis of the idea — and will often read all the smaller stuff before the stories themselves. We like getting little looks into the authors themselves. Fortunately, every contributor not only agreed to drafting up a couple of short lists, but did so with such enthusiasm, fun and humor they made our dorkiness seem like a good idea.

The other interesting aspect of the issue is that it is a double. A kind of literary siamese twin. We have worked, on a number of different occasions with Monkeybicycle, with mutual support and good-natured sibling rivalry, so this is our conjoinment. Our way to show each other off and offer you something original. We hope you enjoy everything about the issue as much as we do. It really was a pleasure to work on.

HOBART
-Aaron

JOHN LEARY

John Leary lives in San Francisco and no longer throws rocks at girls. His stories have appeared or will soon appear in print in *Night Train*, *Pindeldyboz*, *Sweet Fancy Moses*, and the *Ginko Tree Review*. Another story was first runner up in the Missouri Review Editor's Prize and will appear in the *Gettysburg Review* in Spring '04. He does not think he sees himself as others see him, and he is frequently frustrated by issues of stain removal.

likes

Uigurs, bacon sandwiches, ponytails on females, Astrud Gilberto, Calliope Stephanides, nouns, Manny Mota, tacos, spit, Eric Gagne, "to fester," John Doe's voice, citing obscure jazz albums in "likes" recitations, Sue Brooks, flying dreams, Ben Kingsley in "Sexy Beast," the smell of giraffes, "Visitors" by Donald Barthelme, Grace Paley, Kingsley Amis, the idea that stories sit out there in the forest and all you have to do is simply walk in the right direction for a little while, perhaps crossing through bracken, and you will stumble across them (nearly tripping over them, but only nearly) and they will jump into your lap and you will take them home and feed them sugared milk and nurse them into specificity and then you send them off to school only to find that one day when you come home from work that they have disappeared, run away, but not before peeing in your shampoo bottles and teaching your pets bad habits. And, happiness.

dislikes

Uniforms, canned goods, algebra, space, ponytails on men, saying "I mean" before my sentences, offices, tattoos, clocks, stuff in my teeth, cholera, essays, mayonnaise, "home offices," balloons, Michael Douglas, that mean guy named Javier at Goofy's Kitchen at Disneyland who told me the wait would be 70 minutes when the woman on the phone promised me we could walk right in, objects, clowns, discharge, cancer, Robin Williams, "secret sauce." And, overalls. Also, the really stupid idea that something good always comes out of death or a tragedy because, at the very least, you've now got some new material.

DADDY

History is always happening, though sometimes it's merely there, like a guest sitting in the corner of your tent not saying anything. Our lives were like that, for a long time. We kicked around in the Yard, living in our tents eating the mung beans we couldn't eat, fixing the Broken Items, bowing our heads as the rain rain rain came down down down. For a while, Hiram was the only one who complained very loudly, though none of the rest of us would characterize our existence as favored.

Daddy lived in the House with the Wives. The Yard was our place. We had gripes, but we also had agendas. We had factionalized, expertly.

Most days, Lucky plucked his guitar and sang the Song of the Yard:

The Yard, our Yard, our home our friend
There's nothing that's broken that we can't mend
The Gold Book forever will be our guide
We wear our capes and sing with pride
For we're all Daddy's children deep down inside...

The skies were nearly always blue and sunny in Lucky's songs, even though most days rain was our existence: pelting down, crashing down, dribbling and petering and splashing down, falling on our thin scabby heads in the simple way that rain falls.

One day one of the Wives told us that we were not all his kids. Daddy had fourteen or fifteen Wives, each one of them named Mike. Or their names were all pronounced "mike" but each name was spelled differently. It was Mai'ke that told us about Daddy. The Wives come out the Back Door on occasion, sometimes doing friction laundry, sometimes doing steam chores, other times delivering the mung beans and bandages, but most often dropping Broken Items out on the back porch for us to fix.

Mai'ke bounced out of the Back Door on Aid Day and told us. Mai'ke was handing out mung beans and bandages and she said it casually, though most of us suspect there was no way that it was anything but premeditated, the result of some schism or factionalizing within the House. She said, "You know, not all of you are actually Daddy's children… you know that, right?"

She said this to Lilly, our spindly representative with hair blonde as daylight, the favorite child. To her credit, Lilly's grim smile stayed fixed as she said, "Of course, of course. We know that." And when the coast was clear, Lilly sprang away to tell all of us, stray mung beans scattering like beads from a broken necklace.

That night we convened a council in the Main Tent, meeting together for the first time since the Medical Reports. The council met irregularly; we called ourselves The League of Daddy's Children, and it encompassed all of us who lived in the Yard. We numbered 176 persons, 172 boys and four girls. We had believed we were all his children, even if we were carelessly named: he seemed to have scattered names among us like birdseed. How else do you account for five boys named Phyllis? Maik tells us that's a girl's name.

The information Mai'ke had imparted was a horrible revelation, a screech across the record of history, a tear in the weft of things. We accepted the information as fact — deceit was not a big feature of our landscape in the Yard.

We argued whether to change the name of our League, in light of the new information. After a lot of debate, we voted to keep the name.

It seemed there should be some other way to respond to the new information. A few of us were in favor of drafting an encyclical and delivering it via the Wives on Aid Day. Then we started arguing and agendas came to the fore, things that had nothing to do with whether we were truly Daddy's children or not.

Discontent was everywhere, sometimes buried, sometimes hanging like heavy fruit from the trees that the Gold Book tells us once shaded our Yard. As if out of vacant air, discontent came like a plain fact.

Hiram was the most radical. He proposed an elegant solution: "Ah'm ginnae kill the bastard." Hiram spoke with a Scottish accent because he'd watched the video of *Trainspotting* several hundred times.

A few of us protested, to which Hiram responded, "'E dinnae dae shite aboot the Medical Reports, and this is jist another way ay mashin er faces innit. Who's wi ma, den?"

From what we had heard, Daddy ate only mung beans. We, however, were supposed to eat black beans or pintos, but he never gave us any of those. We were not supposed to eat mung beans. We had a note from our clinician. The clinician said it was a dietary impossibility, which is one gradation up from a dietary restriction. There is a shortage (or an excess — we can never remember), of lecithin and other Essential Nutrients in mung beans, so they caused us to suffer gas and hives and sores. Daddy and the Wives noticed the hives and sores, and were kind enough to donate bandages along with the basket of mung beans on the weekly Aid Day. But that wasn't good enough, so we had our clinician's associated practitioner prepare the Medical Reports. Lilly hand-delivered them to Mikke, who promised us they would get directly to Daddy. The next Aid Day, nothing was any different. Mung beans again. We didn't even receive more bandages.

That caused grumbling and muttering which lasted for weeks. During the council, Hiram tried to galvanize the grumbles into gumption. As the council progressed, it seemed that he had to argue a little more than he had expected. Apparently he had expected unanimity.

Dissent to Hiram's enmity bled into the council, embodied by Lucky. A few voices, meek in timbre, joined Lucky's.

One such voice said, "Daddy gave us the Tents, which keep out most of the rain. And he gave us the capes. The Gold Book says that back in the Teen days, the Children all lived in flung-mud huts, which melted in every storm. And no one had any capes."

Hiram had an answer to everything: "The Gold Book also sais the Yard wis a forested land, ken? Now thar's only the Lone Tree. What of that?"

"But under Daddy we have received years of uninterrupted prosperity," came another protest.

"Fie on ye and yer Pax Pater!" Hiram said.

"But what about all the good things about Daddy?" someone asked.

"Like whit?"

"Well, he taught us to sing…"

"Aye, okay, he did dae that. But singins never healed yer sores, whit's ailin ye, 'as it?"

"And the movies, the videos the Wives slip into the mung bean basket on Aid Days. *Three Cops and a Monkey II* is actually pretty good."

"For ev'ry blasted video, yer losin' room for more beans, which you cannae eat anyway!"

"He gave us the keychain pendants, you can't deny that."

"Aye, but he dinnae give ye no fuckin KEYS!"

Many of us shouted our loud assent, then Lucky spoke. He gave a long and impassioned speech, reasoned yet poetic, the gist of it was that we should not rush into anything. We should get more facts. We should begin a dialogue. We shouldn't jump to conclusions. He ended saying, "We know some things, but our ignorance is like another star, not even visible to the naked eye: we don't even know what we don't know. Let us not upset things, and be safe and clean. At least the Yard is ours."

We all turned and looked out past the tent flaps at our rainy puddly smelly Yard. The Gold Book said it was once a land of tiny deer.

Hiram didn't seem to have a response to Lucky. He said, "Whit aboot his dong, eh? The Daddy dong stickin oot the winder on Friday nights when he's got a snootful wi cider and he's pissing down innae holes in yer tent, Lilly? What aboot that, then?"

We burst into shouts of rage. We all loved Lilly. We knew that the piss stung her sores. She had the sweetest voice of all of us — when she would sing one of Lucky's songs as he strummed the guitar we would nearly forget the rain.

It is a sad fact of our existence in the Yard, an existence with no means of voice amplification, that he who shouts loudest is often deemed to be the correctest. Lucky started to speak again but Hiram shouted him down with curses. Hiram stood up before us all and yelled that if Lucky was going to sit back and allow things to continue as they had, then Lucky was a cur, a nappy-wearing trog, an unpatriotic git, a poncy arse, a bloody tosser. And the curses seemed to work. No one else who had voiced any dissent seemed to want to be called those names.

Only a few of us know how a laser works, but we can all imagine that it must work something like what we saw around Hiram then: his rage and hatred bounced off all of us as if we were mirrors and grew stronger, sharper, brighter, until it funneled and fused through Hiram into a tight ray of white light, sharp and keen as justice.

Hiram said, "Aye. What aboot a vote, then?"

Nearly everyone agreed: yes, it was time to vote.

But Lucky was not done. He shook with fear and rage and shame and insecurity. He had held a hill he thought it was his moral duty to hold, and watched as all potential allies fled to the enemy camp. Seeming to strain at the sinews, he said, "What about the Gold Book? Doesn't it say something about this? Shouldn't we look in the Gold Book?"

No one wanted to say what many of us were thinking: getting the Gold Book down from the Holy Shelf and taking it out of its Plastic Wrapper wouldn't tell us anything — the Gold Book is just a symbol, full of words, and anyone who believed in words at times like these was an idiot.

However, it seemed that Hiram had only been waiting for someone to ask. When the Gold Book was removed and ready, Hiram seized it, and flipped to a page he must have known was there, and read:

Whosoever shall cause the suffering of the Children, shall also feel the sting of their rage; let mercy not be his catacomb but his tomb.

That seemed to settle it. Lucky hung his head.

Nothing focuses things like an enemy. The word enemy tastes like dirt against the teeth. Without an enemy, life can go limp.

Then Hiram did something brilliant. He announced a scale-back of his idea. It was brilliant because it looked like a conciliation; it made us all look less radical, and arrayed us all (except Lucky) completely behind him. He said, "We don' have tae kill him, ken? If'n yer not sure we can jist dae a trap."

"Yes!" We shouted. "A trap!"

"We vote!" Hiram announced. "All in favor ay a trap, say 'Aye!'"

The ayes had it. Lucky was the lone nay vote.

"Great." Hiram exulted. "It'll be jist like the movies."

Then he said, "Yer aw makin history, ken?"

Then he said, "Tae show yer unity, from now, all capes er red."

This is how we implemented the first stage of plan, the Trap: we stopped fixing the Broken Items. Soon they started to pile up on the porch near the Back Door. A razor scooter, a stackable washer/dryer combo, a DVD player, an electric candelabra, a Wonderbra, an electronic singing Santa Claus — we just left them there, listing against each other in the rusting rain.

Some of us couldn't stand seeing the Broken Items piled and unattended to. If we weren't fixing the Broken Items, we were mostly idle. One of the Phyllises, a master of electrical engineering, was caught tinkering with the broken DVD player one night, and Hiram directed that he be banished to his tent.

When Daddy finally came outside, he didn't look as we had expected him to look. We'd heard of a huge Daddy built like John Huston in *Chinatown*, who would cause the sun to blaze off his bald dome and blind us. We'd heard Daddy's eyes had grown weak; we'd heard of his epic corpulence. We'd heard he was so fat and bald that his brow sagged down over his eyes. We'd heard he used toothpicks covered in felt to prop up the two mini-sausages of his brow to allow him to see. But when he stepped out on the front porch to see Lilly, he actually looked pretty good. Not Tom Cruise-good, but not bad. Better than Tom Arnold, for example. He was taller than any of us, by at least two feet. Whether he was bigger than normal or we were smaller, we have no idea, as we have no way of knowing what normal is.

Our new strategy had made Daddy come out. When there was no hubbub about the unfixed Broken Items, when the bean baskets and bandage racks continued to come on Aid Day, we adopted a new strategy. We used Lilly. We spread word to the Wives that Lilly was sick to the point of dying. We placed her mock-festering body there on the back porch, and waited.

Daddy came out and looked at Lilly. Most of us had never seen him before.

Who knows why he came out? He may have been motivated by mercy or compassion, or the need to gloat or to wave his glory over us. Or curiosity, or sadness. Ultimately, the emotion is not as important as the fact, because everyone has a different interpretation of the emotion and the facts are less refutable.

The fact that he picked Lilly up and "cradled" her is pretty irrefutable, though some say there was no cradling; that he picked her up like trash to get her off the porch, looking for a place to chuck her seeping body, her skin dappled with sores and scabs. Others say he, without a thought of contagion or infection cradled her in his arms and sunk his face into her few remaining strands of golden hair. Those same people saw tears drip from Daddy.

Then he turned as if maybe to take her inside with him but she pointed No, there, down there, among the tents. It wasn't clear what she said to him, though it is clear that he took two steps forward, stepping right into the inertia skates. He must have felt himself stepping into the skates, because he looked down — but of course he was holding Lilly, so he could not see his feet. Instead, he saw Lilly peeling off her cellophane skin on which we had painted seeping sores, peeling it away like a *Mission Impossible* mask. Then the fun began.

Before Daddy had time to react to what he surely must have suspected was danger, she delivered her line: "Hasta la vista, Dadeee!"

A hundred arms then tugged the ropes attached to the pulleys hung high in the Lone Tree and the translucent wires attached to Lilly tightened and she flew from Daddy's grasp, shooting toward the sky then stopping and hovering just beyond his reach like Kim Greist in front of Jonathan Pryce in *Brazil*. Behind her, the earth erupted into a bloom of red — we were all, all 175 of us, wearing red capes, which we twirled like torreadors, flashing with flair.

As Lilly fluttered before him, Daddy, probably against his better judgment, leaned forward. The skates lost their hold, and Daddy cascaded forward and down along the crude track we had built until he smashed his toes into the pile of bricks, and pitched forward into the blue cotton sheet hanging from the bandage racks set atop a small platform. The blue cotton sheet was coated on both sides with a wonder adhesive, and as Daddy flailed in the grasp of the sheet, his momentum caused him to tumble off the platform and land face first in the two plastic children's swimming pools we had cut and laid end to end. The pools were filled with hair and feathers, which immediately clung to all sides of the blue cotton sheet as Daddy struggled and roared. The twelve members of the Red Cape Brigade ringed the pools, each member holding a metal squeeze can of charcoal lighter fluid, which they spritzed onto Daddy as he struggled to stand.

The Red Cape Brigade parted to allow Hiram to stand at the edge of the pools. Hiram nonchalantly used one hand to expose his metal fly, and the other hand to strike a blue-tip match across the fly. He tossed the lit match at Daddy, just as Daddy regained his feet and stood.

Burning Daddy! Burning Daddy!

Hiram had written a burning Daddy song, which many of us sang:

Rip your eyes out screaming Daddy!
Wail and turn and flail!
Burn like hell you naughty baddie!
Your thunder falls like hail!
Beee-caaaaaa -uuuussse. . . .
There's naught that you can do
O, there's naught that you can do
'Cause the burning's held on with Su--per Glue!

And there's a little dance that went with it, too.

Burning blazing Daddy stumbled and tottered then ran as best he could with his legs glued and tangled, storming through our warren of tents. He dove into the fishpond, which apparently we'd forgotten about. He killed twelve koi and badly seared two frogs.

For a minute everyone was silent; the only sound was the hiss of the steam coming from the pond. We looked at each other quickly: Is he dead? Is he drowning?

Then Daddy rose from the pond. Still steaming, covered in patches of charred sheet and blackened flesh and burnt bits, bloody and raw and smoking and steaming, he rose slowly like Martin Sheen in *Apocalypse Now*. He straightened up to his enormous Daddy-height and stepped from the pond then wagered an unsteady walk back toward the House.

He was midway to the Back Door when Hiram blocked his path. Many of us were shocked at the horror, the screams, all the misery and burning we'd seen. But apparently for Hiram, the job was not yet done.

Hiram stepped into Daddy's path and Daddy stopped his smoldering tread. Brave and terrified Hiram stood there, holding before him the only weapon we possessed: a corkscrew he held with two hands, like Patricia Arquette in *True Romance*.

Daddy spoke first. "How could you be so stupid? You forgot about the fishpond?"

Hiram, trembling but steeling himself, shrugged.

Daddy said, "That was a massive failure of intelligence!"

Hiram flared his nostrils and seemed as if he was about to give a great answer, a great speechified answer. Before he could do so, the Hand of Daddy rose up and blotted out the rain. The Hand hung there at its apex a moment, made a fist, and the fist came crashing down like Fury, like Hate, like the opposite of Mercy, right down squarely in the middle of Hiram's skull.

From off to the side, Lucky began to sing a song about the death of Hiram; it seemed he had already written it and practiced it:

'E was just a wee bairn
Now we build his cairn
Forgettin' our Daddy
Can beat any laddie . . .

Hiram should have been dead, and maybe he was dead, but there was something like special effects that happened next: Daddy's hand made a squishing blopule sound as it passed through Hiram, and Hiram split and the two Hiram sides flopped wetly to the ground.

Everyone gasped.

Then suddenly the two halves moved and throbbed then beaded into multi-colored puddles and then from each puddle sprang a new Hiram, looking exactly like the old Hiram, except slightly smaller.

It looked just like something out of *The Matrix*. Or *Terminator 2*. "Oooooooooh! Cooooooooool!" we all said.

Each of the two Hirams held a teensy sword. Probably it was the serious burns Daddy had suffered all over his body, probably it was also the shock of seeing the Hirams; but Daddy reeled, Daddy staggered, and Daddy toppled, falling backwards onto the puddly soil of the Yard, raising a splash and a hiss of steam as the last fires on his body were extinguished.

The Hirams looked puzzled for a moment, then one of them jumped over to Lucky, and with a swoop and a flourish worthy of a Musketeer movie, serrated Lucky roughly across the midsection, nearly cutting him in two.

“Heh!" said that Hiram, wiping his sword on his leg, “Looks like mibbe yer luck has run oot!”

Then they both moved toward Daddy. They probably would have killed him next if two of the Wives, Meick and Mmike, hadn’t rushed out the Back Door and pulled Daddy into the House.

Daddy had let us listen to whatever songs we wanted. “Rock Me Tonight,” “Tonight I’m Gonna Rock,” “Me and You Rockin’ Tonight,” were some of our favorites. The videos we received from the House were more varied, in hindsight, than we thought at the time we agreed to do the Trap. Yes, we saw every movie in the *Cop and a Monkey* series. We saw every one from *Cop and a Monkey I*, continuing with the five sequels and prequel series all the way to *Return of Three Cops and a Monkey IV*. We saw those movies the most, because those were the movies we liked the most, and we think Daddy knew that. But there were other movies, like *Mystery Train* or *Orlando* or *The Road Warrior*, and we watched them too.

The Hirams have a different entertainment agenda. They only allow us to listen to two songs: “Boogie with Stu” and “Waterfalls.”

One of the Hirams has grown a little beard, to distinguish himself from the other Hiram. The Hiram of the beard has asked to be called “Fergus.” Most of us continue to refer to them as “the Hirams.” They want us to make our own entertainment, to end our reliance on Daddy. They’ve taken spare bandages and made hundreds of sock puppets, encouraging us to put on shows. The puppets lie in a corner of the yard, damp.

Nearly every day, the Hirams take a poll. A poll is, they remind us with an uninfectious laugh, very different from a vote. Every Aid Day, they give a speech.

A new faction has formed and the Hirams watch it warily, panning their sharp eyes over to the rice paddy that was once the fish-pond. That's where the Phyllises gather. The new faction is led by one of the Phyllises and includes two other Phyllises. We think the Hirams use their polls to measure how they are doing in relation to the Phyllises.

The Phyllises were the first to turn their capes inside out, so the red is on the inside, and the normal, pre-Trap navy blue is on the outside. Lately, many capes in the Yard are worn this way, the most common explanation being that the red side soils more easily.

Each Aid Day, a Wife brings mung beans and bandages, as before. The Wife making the delivery is usually Meik, the youngest and slimmest of the Wives, and sometimes she speaks to us. The Broken Items no longer appear on the back porch.

Even with little contact from the Wives, we hear rumors about Daddy. We hear he's on life support now, spending nine hours each day lying in a bathtub filled with a hibiscus sherbet balm that heals burns. When he gets up to conduct his business, he's wrapped in cucumber and jojoba-salved bandages. Theories abound among us explaining what "jojoba" might smell like. We hear Daddy spends several hours in a dry-mist room, bandages off, each day to allow his burns to breathe.

Every single one of us expects retribution. We're not sure in what form it will come. We only hear more rumors: robot dogs made of kevlar and glass fiber with clamping jaws will storm the Yard. We will be issued exploding cell phones. Slowly we will become aware of a gray goo that chews our tents and turns our mud puddles into mini-pits of fire. We've heard the Wives have organized themselves into a Strike Force with nightscopes, so Hiram has posted regular guards in the evenings to watch over the Yard.

The Hirams do some leading; they seem to think they are our leaders, but they seem disappointed in our halfhearted fervor. We are pretty sure that on the day of the Trap we had believed what we believed. It may look sort of bad today, but it turns out that many of us didn't really hold our beliefs so tightly after all. That is not to say that beliefs are mutable things, but more that they are like a book, and some of us — most of us, probably — had only read the first few pages.

One of the Phyllises has learned to play Lucky's guitar, and has composed a song called the Daddy dirge:

Who could forget our Daddy?
Who could forget our Daaaaaaaa-aaaaddy?
In his footpuddle treads we sailed our boats
His generousness we wore like coats
Our sorrow knows no end
Our sorrow knows no end
We hang our heads in shame
For we were Daddy's bane

The Hirams have banned this song; some of us hum it nonetheless. Without the Broken Items to repair, we've lost some focus. Each day arrives in a measured portion: two meals of mung beans and rice, and an evening viewing of *Il Postino* or *Trainspotting*, the only videos the Hirams allow us to watch.

Each Aid Day, one of us accepts the mung beans and bandages from Meik and then transfers them to Fergus. Fergus gives them to Hiram, who ascends the small dais he's built from the remains of the plastic pools and ramp, and addresses us prior to the doling of the beans.

The rain rain rain continues to come down down down, and there's a brown spot on the grass where Lilly fell. We're not sure what she had been trying to do. Maybe she had been trying to hold Daddy and allow the Hirams to get him. Maybe she had been trying to protect him from the Hirams. In any event, when Daddy toppled backward, Lilly was behind him, and he crushed her into a damp powder.

Retribution is coming, we know that. The Hirams have told us to be wary of the forms it takes. Some days Meik will come down to the back porch and tell us things. The Hirams tell us she is the most dangerous form of retribution, but we can't help ourselves.

She sits and we gather around her and she tells us about things we don't know, things we don't learn from the songs or the videos: urban sprawl, pop-art, irrational exuberance, entrepreneurship, the smell of a new harpsichord and the primacy of the individual.

Today Hiram stood on the dais and spoke of the continuing struggle against Daddy. He told us that the battle we are fighting is one of ideologies, that it is not necessary to defeat, to kill Daddy, but rather to triumph over the *idea* of Daddy, to triumph over all he stands for.

The other Hiram, Fergus, moved among the crowd, taking an insta-poll. After a few queries, he looked up at Hiram and shook his head: the notion of triumph over ideology, over the idea of Daddy, wasn't very catchy.

Some nights we can hear a dull thocking noise coming from the middle of the Yard where the Lone Tree stands. It is Hiram, people whisper, pounding his head against the tree trunk, trying to split in two again.

Two days ago Meik brought us a jar marked "BBQ." The jar was filled with a delicious red substance that moved many of us to tears. She has promised us she will get us something called "mint chocolate chip ice cream," and some of us are so excited with speculation that we can't sleep.

Maybe they are dangerous, these things she is telling us and giving us. But their allure is undeniable, pulling more strongly than any edict from the Hirams.

Hiram saw Fergus' headshake and seemed to reconsider. He seemed to realize that there are places that the warm light of reason cannot reach. He looked over toward the Phyllises. Finally he said,

"Ow aboot this then: the House! Dae ye wannae conquer the House?"

"Yes! The House! The House! Someday, we will conquer the House!" a few people said, but most of us lowered our heads and shuffled over to collect our mung bean ration.

Why weren't we more excited? We have unrolled the scroll of history and danced upon it. We have made our mark. Maybe we realize that for many years we will all be remembered, then over time only the Hirams will be remembered, then even the Hirams will be forgotten. Everything dies.

Sometimes an ending, a finality, a closure, all of those things that cleave a line into the bloody continuum of history and say yes, humanity is starting over and what has happened before has no bearing on what has happened again, is impossible. In a way, at least, it's impossible. In another way it's the easiest thing in the world, because the end of history is always now.

Meik has taught us about male pattern baldness, mussels, the care and feeding of a chia-pet, manifest destiny, irony, tropes, spangles, and stop-loss orders. Life is disappointing, she teaches us. Life is full of disappointment and life is sad. So she says the key is to watch movies (her favorite is *Thunderball*) and sample different sauces.

Today she told us that tomorrow she will teach us about cynicism. The Hirams have vowed to stop her.

Lee Klein

Lee Klein edits Eyeshot.net

likes

Antediluvian dictionaries with hundreds of thousands of skin-thin pages; Vintage lemon-lime seltzer; Miller High Life commercials; Nico's "Chelsea Girl" in October, Jorge Ben's "Africa Brasil" in July, The Sea & Cake's "The Biz" in May, The Microphone's "The Glow Pt 2" in January; the thoughts that come from sunset clouds seen from airborne airplanes; the endorphins that come from running through woods in Iowa City's Hickory Hill Park; the laughs that come when a car of toughs smoking blunts pulls up to a small crowd smoking cigarettes outside a Brooklyn bar & one tough in the car asks if anyone has "their personal paintings" on the walls of the bar & a friend yanks up his t-shirt & twists around to reveal a huge tattoo of an oak tree on his back & says "I got your personal paintings right here, buddy;" eel handroll; Iverson, McKie, & Snow; ostriches; puppycats; all the world when the world's not insane.

dislikes

When the neighbor's Eminem-wannabe friends' souped-up Hondas blast 50 Cent & perpetuate urban stereotypes outside my window while I try to read the tender-and-elusive shit; postprandial hypotension; the dozens of thousands of feet between airborne airplanes & the ground; any idea not at one point expressed on "The Simpson's," idiotic fuckhead evildoers, especially those who misrepresent our country's amber waves & purple majesty; the somewhat short arms of the Irish (compare them with the arms of Spaniards or Poles!); not spending enough time skinny-skiing or going to bullfights on acid; asymmetrical nipple protrusion through sheer summertime fabric; arguments reducing baseball's complexity and beauty to payroll size; days when nothing gets done 'cause the previous night went way too long; wintertime weeks when the sun's never seen; when the central seam down the back of a lady's denim skirt slides toward either cheek; when I pay too much attention to what I dislike.

Brave Men Run

She walks out of the airport terminal bathroom, her posture worthy of balancing sacks of grain on her head. She looks around where she last saw me. I've hidden myself behind a soda machine. I just barely catch a glance. She doesn't seem abandoned. She stops, stands still. I have her half-packed duffel tucked out of sight. She's alone in the Philadelphia airport with only what she has in her pockets. She stands there, a solid figure just a few strides in front of the women's bathroom. A barely perceptible glow on the side of her cheek. I'd jump out if I sensed distress. But she just stands there, not moving, probably expecting me to emerge from the men's room any second. She reaches into her well-worn jeans, pulls out a dollar, tries to smooth it on her thigh. Then she uses the edge of a pay-phone encasement, working over the creases in Washington's portrait until he looks much younger, more amendable to the soda machine's discerning dollar-bill mechanism. She starts moving toward me. I duck back against the wall. Then I realize it'd be better if I continued observing from point-blank range. I position myself so a sliver of my eye can just see the least outline of her jacket. I hear the dollar-bill mechanism inhale her bill. A moment of choice. She presses one of the rectangular glowing logos. I feel the soda machine's internal mechanisms process her order. There's a second between her pressing and the drop of the can, a hesitancy, and in that second I wonder if the machine's considering whether it should honor its side of the bargain (since it already has the money), or maybe there's something else going on: like it's thinking how can I give *this one* a can of my precious soda? I feel a glass-hanging moment of potential rejection that shatters when the can drops. I peek around and see her squaring her back to the machine, probably thinking I'm in the men's room cleansing my digestive tract of inorganic build up, that I should really get on with it. I pounce out from my blind, with the strap of her duffel diagonally bisecting my chest, and grab an orb of her buttocks. She whirls. Not like a pirouetting ballerina, not with lots of swift graceful movement and readying of limbs for a crushing retort. But rather, *she turns*. There isn't much to it. She turns, reaches around, and casually grabs a handful of my ass.

"I saw you there all along," she accuses.

I charge my eyes with purpose, stare as deeply as I can into her head, and say slowly, "No… you… didn't."

"I… did… not… see… you," she says, as though hypnotized. Then she breaks our tight connection, hands me a Mountain Dew. "Looks like you could use this," she says

I thought I had her. But she would never drink Mountain Dew. She ordered for me.

I crack open the can.

She gives me a screwy look like *how the hell can you drink that stuff?*

I take a big sip, hold it, then try kissing her. I want to release the fizzing contents of my cheeks into hers. But she rejects it. Jerks away. Mocks my silliness.

I haven't seen her for months, not since just before the beginning of summer. Not since we kissed goodbye on my hometown New Jersey porch after she rescued me from a situationally shitty two years in Boston, where I'd lived a corrosively loveless life. Now we're at the Philadelphia airport. She flew from North Carolina to visit her brother, a young man my age she's described in superhero terms. He's a man of steel. Spinach-packed forearms. The total package. He's benignly high-strung, jacked-up on positivity, a walking inspiration, an invigorating source. Someone who raises the level of talk and action. Who challenges everyone's evils in a way that is not malicious, but messianic. That's the way the sister describes the brother. It's a character study in perfection. I imagine him in vibrant leotard and cape, donning an action-belt of superhero gadgets, vapor-cloud release grenades and such: things that ease exits from tricky situations.

But Hannah spices her report about her brother. She admits to fraternal abuse, youthful pestering, sibling teasing, repeated annoyances. The constant teasing would break her down fifteen years ago, but now she realizes he expressed his love by pestering her. And when she considers Francis as he is, volunteering at a northwestern New Jersey organic farm with another Oregon-bred friend, raising crops out of the impossibly fertile soil of the Garden State (now that her memory is almost sacred and he has ascended to something more than a brother), she thinks of the fact that he once took pleasure in making her cry, and she does more than forgive: she considers her tears and the now-healed hurt as artifacts, relics of their time together.

It was sunny this morning when I left my parents' house in New Jersey. But now, in Philadelphia, it's overcast. With the strap of her bag still in place, we cross the street into Area C of the airport parking lot. My old hatchback wagon receives her cargo. She climbs in. I'm giddy. I start talking: "What's odd is that, first thing this morning, my mom told me how my grandfather, her father — this blind Polish guy I saw once when I was fifteen; he said when I was born, 'That's all we need, another Jew bastard,' even though I could never be officially Jewish because my mom's Catholic — my mom told me this morning that my grandfather, her father, got in a bar fight when he was about my age. Killed a guy, then spent ten years hiding out in Poland. The first thing he did when he came back to Newark was knock up my grandmother — who died before I was born — knocked her up with my mom. I never heard about that 'til this morning. So I was thinking about it as I drove to the airport."

"Shouldn't you start the car?"

"Right — I mean, I've been thinking about that bar fight. That one of my grandfathers, that *my progenitor* killed a man. And get this, the fight was supposedly over my grandfather buying a round of drinks at a neighborhood bar. This is like in the 1930s, mid-

Depression, immigrant-addled Newark, long before my mother was born. Supposedly this guy was giving my grandfather grief for standing a round of drinks for everyone at the bar instead of taking the money home to his wife and my mom's older brother. My grandfather let the guy know he wasn't interested in suggestions about how to live his life. It got bloody, and continued to get bloodier, and bloodier, until that guy giving my granddaddy grief was dead."

"Do you need money for the parking?"

"I got it. But it's hard to imagine, right? Just like that, my grandfather kills a man, and instead of enjoying his drink at the bar, or taking care of his family, he's escaping across the Atlantic, stowing away, deep into his homeland for ten years, before he returns to begin my mom's life. Crazy, huh? I learned that this morning."

"Why did your mom wait so long to tell you?"

"She was just thinking… I don't know. Maybe she thinks escaping runs in the family."

"You haven't killed anyone."

"But still, it's kind of like I'm exiling myself as if I had. Killed someone… My mom was asking how you felt about all this business about my leaving for South America. She was lecturing me about how I wasn't considering your feelings. How it must be hard. About how little I seem to be thinking about you."

Hannah's silent as we make it out of the airport parking lot. On I-95 North following signs to Trenton, merging into Philadelphia highway traffic, avoiding trucks, side-swept Chevrolets, cars with at least twenty years of service logged in body damage. "Love of Brother" rendered in tall toxic reeds snorkeling up from the shit-green Schuylkill; rusted iron infrastructure with now unidentifiable functions; an industrial plant being demolished by a slow wrecking ball so the ruin looks like a cathedral designed by Gaudi (everything collapsing on itself); billboards for rock radio stations, for whiskies, for casinos, for gentleman's clubs, for detoxification clinics — one billboard with the Camel logo centered in the middle of a hypnotic spiral of green-and-orange smoke. Billboards colonizing rectangles of sky, distracting attention from the road.

Three wide, pockmarked lanes. I take the center. Steady at fifty-five. Ahead of us in the right lane, a car is clipped across the front fender. It spins in a complete circle, halts, then continues to chase the car that cut it off and exited the highway.

"I can't believe no one pulled over," Hannah says, her right hand cupping her forehead as though the accident were too bright.

"This is Philly," I explain, feeling like a post-apocalyptic tour guide. "It's like a videogame. You crash, recover, then hurry to make up lost ground."

"It's so cloudy," Hannah says minutes later, rightly emphasizing the obvious. Clouds over northeastern Philadelphia naturally absorb menace.

"It wasn't this morning in New Jersey," I answer.

"It's *never* cloudy in New Jersey," she says, and I can feel her staring at me, smiling, accusing me of regional zeal, as I watch the road, tightly navigating the whitewater leading away from the city and into the provincial seas and bays.

"You're so proud of New Jersey. But you're only there to make enough money to leave it for a few years."

I'm sure she means *leave me for a few years*.

We pass the old prison's walls and watchtowers, the Oxford Valley Mall, Sesame Place. I take the Yardley exit and head along the Pennsylvania side of the Delaware River. I tell her the foliage is dense because it's a temperate jungle. There are ferns along the floor and kudzu-like vines webbing through the trees. I'm gawking at the density of nature, seeing it all with her eyes, the way I would want her to see it (inspired and overawed, thrilled with where-I'm-from, as proud of my natural habitat as I am).

She thinks I'm silly.

A dork.

I am.

I tell her I know.

That I can't help it.

I want her to marvel.

She tells me to relax.

We chug past Flemington's new car lots and their hundred-yard American flags that cover huge quadrants of brand-new automobiles in billowing shadow. My wagon strains itself on the inclines and rattles downhill. I'm thinking that an emergency trade-in might be necessary to get me home after I drop off Hannah with her brother. We'll be early. Francis expects us at five. It's not even three-thirty yet. I pull off the road at a little rural town called Butzville. Could be anywhere in New England or the South, with streams and a simple, rustic, nearly abandoned bridge. It's warm. I park the car. We lean against the rusted railing of the bridge. The rocks in the swift shallow water seem to struggle upstream without any progress. Hannah rests against me. Kissing as though we're perfect. I'll leave soon. Now I'm with her. It's perfect here. On this bridge in Butzville. There is no way we can mention the future. It's perfect: kissing on a bridge in Butzville. We're both dressed in complimentary earth-tones, for fuck's sake. The sun is a diamond, the sky its setting. We are the… I don't know what. I have a destination in mind.

Hannah says nothing. There's a sweetness. Seductive, honest emotion. She's taking a solid glance before steadying herself. Her eyes preparing for regret. There's something at once funereal and celebratory: the day is perfect when it should be dismal. And we're together, maybe for the last time. We decide not to talk about it. Not even to agree to keep quiet. We'll be silent. Not grind things down with words.

Francis' organic farm is just outside of a town called Hope, just after what he calls "The thickest sycamore in New Jersey." We find the farm without a problem, trail dust down a long gravel road, pass the tee-pees where Francis and his friend sleep. Then we see the fields: lush, radiant, rolling hills covered in crops that defy my definitions, things hidden beneath the soil, rows of this and that — crops she can identify either from instinct or the way her brother planted them. We see two silhouettes at the top of a hill in the long shadow-casting sun. It's like something out of Millet, with those rounded idealized forms, except these are interactive. Francis and his friend see us park, and when we start walking toward them, they come at us, attacking with tomatoes. I catch a few cleanly and hurl them back in one fluid jai-alai-type movement. They weren't expecting a counter attack. They're doing the old lob-and-fire tactic that's so useful in snowball fights. But with seed-heavy, splattery tomatoes, the attack's more like a welcome to their agrarian lunacy, a hard-working island of cultivation and wholesomeness — something to which I've never applied and could never join. And when Hannah sits on her hams, spitting out the seeds of just-plucked grapes in a way that could only be called *languorous* (the four of us sitting in a semi-circle on a hill of long grass, after establishing a tomato truce), I understand that this is her habitat. She knows the mannerisms, the speech, the subsistence-farmer lingo: a well-educated populism streaked through with stream of consciousness, a sort of quirky beatitude covering all bases and food groups with vegetative swarms of thought.

Francis is not a superhero. He's short, hairy-chested, hook-nosed; his forearms, like Popeye's, are absolutely misproportioned to his height. He doesn't live up to the hype. But I'm intimidated by something, maybe the late-afternoon light. When I speak I hear my voice disappearing. I try to muster confidence, but I don't have it. Francis' friend hitchhiked across America from farm to farm. He's at least two inches taller than me, naked except for rotting purple overalls and a soggy newspaper delivery-boy bag full of tomatoes. He's scarecrow thin, has a scraggily beard, wears old-school Converse hightops with the sides cut-out for ventilation. When this guy asks what I do, Hannah tells him I'm about to go teach English in Peru. She says it and indirectly insults herself. Because I'm not staying with her. Because she's not announcing that we've come to a decision. Because I haven't considered settling with her in Chapel Hill. It's a let-down. A celebration is canceled. The grapes will surely induce terrible runs. My voice is still failing. Hannah is from another world that's steady and generative, a place impossible for me to enter.

My eyes water from hay fever as I swat a fuzzy halo of gnats.

I get ready to leave.

There's nothing more to say.

The lunatic scarecrow disappears without goodbyes. Francis packs me a take-home bag of tomatoes, dozens of jalapeños, every color of pepper, enough produce for a gallon of salsa. Hannah and I move toward my faded blue hatchback. We don't talk. I sit behind the wheel with my sneakers on the gravel. She leans down to kiss me for a few seconds, looking up to see if her brother sees. She walks down the path towards where Francis has gone to pick apples. I watch her walk hundreds of feet down the path as she becomes smaller, periodically waving, until she disappears into a turn.

Soon after I start driving home I see a sign for something called "The Land of Make-Believe." I follow the sign a mile down a side road and turn into the parking lot of a closed-for-the-season water-park. Everything seems ready for business. The waterslides and log-plumes stand out in primary-colored plastic twists against a backdrop of thick foliage beginning to change colors. Only there's no water. No one to enjoy "The Land of Make-Believe," although it's hot enough and the sun's still strong for late October.

On the way home, I stop at a Burger King. I have a Whopper, onion rings, and a large root beer. I sit in the solarium, wondering whether the plants are growing in their pots or if they're florals, easing myself with the texture of fast food: the blend of flame-broiled cow, batter-fried onion, thousand island dressing, nutritionally useless iceberg lettuce, pickle shards. My plastic tray is brown. The radio pumps out a country version of a Supremes hit. I almost giggle tearfully into my meal. I suck down what's left of the spongy air-pumped bun. All of it mixing with bitter saliva, digestive acids processing it slowly, churning the instantly delivered meal into an easily evacuated sludge that has nothing to do with me, that's not related to my mechanisms and therefore can pass (irretrievably) into something larger.

And then I realize that I never saw Hannah take her duffel.

I run to the car, hoping she forgot her bag in my backseat.

She didn't, of course, and I drive home, thinking about making the hottest salsa I possibly can. Something that would really burn.

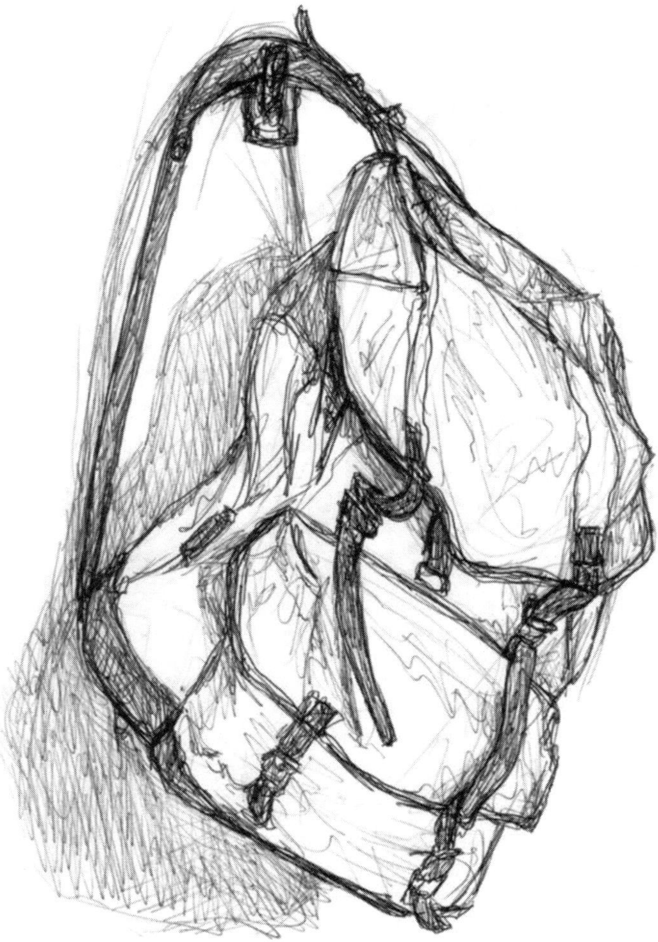

Susan Townsend

Susan B. Townsend is a writer and stay at home mother. Transplanted from the west coast of Canada five years ago, she now makes her home on a 300 acre farm in southeastern Virginia with her husband, five children, and a zoo full of animals. Her work has appeared in *Megaera*, *Wild Violet*, *The Sidewalk's End*, *Moondance*, *Pierian Springs*, *Poor Mojo's Alamanc(k)*, *Ink Magzine*, *The Dead Mule*, *Pindeldyboz*, and *Wired Hearts*. She can be reached at monitor@visi.net.

likes

piles and rows of books, hairless rats, buzzards, praying mantises (Is that the plural?), spiders, Russian and Sulcatta tortoises, Box turtles, white chocolate, blue cheese and strawberry jam sandwiches, ugly antique teddy bears, Matrimonial cake, pizza with pine nuts, spinach, feta cheese, and sundried tomatoes, old ugly sock monkeys, groundhogs, smooth, perfectly round pebbles, tidal pools, people that want you to succeed, being married to my best friend, my first husband, being forgiven, being pregnant, giving birth, being a mother, naps after lunch, electrical storms, old houses and apartments

dislikes

liars, black pakistani cobras, hunting season, starving hunting dogs, livestock trucks carrying hogs, Christmas without my mother and my Aunt Charlotte and Uncle Jack, my second husband (mildly), my third husband (intensely), hamsters and white mice, balancing the cheque book, being forced to eat outdated foods by people who think you're being picky, telephones, the Interstate, people that say, "How nice. What do you write?", people who treat their animals like children and people who treat their children like animals, hurricanes

Family Therapy

On Friday, I allowed a group of strangers to admit my fifteen-year-old son, Ben, to a juvenile psychiatric facility. "It's for his own protection and the well-being of those around him," the doctor told me, making it sound like Ben had leprosy. By the time Monday morning arrived, along with the appointment for our first session, I was still trying to dig myself out from an avalanche of guilt. This kind of thing didn't happen to good mothers. Sons with competent, caring mothers don't take a paring knife and carve up their arms like so much stringy pot roast.

Like a murder trial, my mind dredged up every scrap of evidence — irrefutable proof that I had failed my only child. I remembered when he was three and I slapped his face because he spat at me. And when he was twelve, he said that he hated me. Instead of counting to ten or walking away, I told him I hated him, too.

My defense attorney didn't have a chance. It didn't matter how many times I'd read *The Cat in the Hat* at two in the morning. It didn't matter how many Band-Aids I doled out, for injuries real and imagined, or how many monsters I banished from his closet.

I had tried so hard to check everything off the list that went on forever — the list of things good mothers do. Talking to him even before he even knew what I was saying, listening for hours, pretending to listen when I couldn't anymore, and loving him every moment. Not liking him very much sometimes, but always loving him. I loved him even when I didn't love myself, but something went wrong.

Something slipped by.

I dressed for the appointment with care and a critical eye. Maybe if the packaging looked good, no one would notice the disheveled contents. I appraised my reflection in the bedroom mirror and promised myself I wouldn't babble the way I always did when I was nervous. I'd listen, I'd find out what Ben needed, and I'd do whatever it took. My husband Peter called to me from the kitchen. "We'd better get going."

I glanced at the clock and noticed with some shock that we might actually arrive on time. Punctuality was not one of Peter's strong suits. He must be nervous, too, I decided, but the truth was, I didn't know what demons he battled. I had been too busy sinking into my own quicksand of self-recrimination to ask him how felt. When was the last time Peter and I really talked?

Then, in an unexpected moment of clarity, my self-pity gave way to the realization that, as Ben had grown older, my conversations with him had changed, too, both in frequency and duration. What had I missed as we each took on our subconscious vow of silence?

At five minutes to eleven we walked through the doors faking the confidence of veterans. We provided Ben's identification number, signed in, and clipped on our guest tags. The receptionist gestured to some chairs in the lobby. "Just have a seat," she said. "I'll tell the counselor you're here."

We sank into a large, overstuffed couch, and I ran my hand over the expensive fabric. The lobby reminded me of an overpriced hotel I stayed in a long time ago, but guests at luxury hotels did not have ID numbers, and they weren't separated from their visitors by three locked doors.

The largest weeping fig plant I'd ever seen dominated the room. I got up and approached it for further inspection. It was too perfect — it had to be one of those crappy silk things. "Wow," I said to Peter. "This fig is real. These are hard to grow. Fussy as hell. They must take really good care of it."

He shook his head. "There are companies that grow plants and take them around to offices and places like this. When the plant starts to deteriorate, they replace it."

"Oh," I said and returned to the couch. My vision of the staff nurturing both plants and patients, providing them with a caring, supportive atmosphere and coaxing them into a strong, healthy state, vanished.

I was startled by the sudden appearance of a woman standing in front of me. Like a shield, she clutched a clipboard to her chest. "Hi," she said with a quick tilt of her head. "You must be Mr. and Mrs. Thomas. Ben's parents." We stood up and shook hands. "I'm Christine," she replied. "One of the counselors here."

"How's Ben? Can we see him?" I asked.

She smiled. "He's fine. Of course you can. Follow me."

I pointed to the fig tree as we left the reception area. "That's the most incredible weeping fig I've ever seen."

She gave the tree a quick glance. "Oh," she said. "I've never really noticed it." Okay, I thought. She's probably far too busy with her patients to notice a seven-foot tall, five-foot wide plant that she passes at least twice a day.

Ben's face lit up when he saw us, and he hurried over. "I might get to go home today," he whispered, his voice trembling with excitement.

Peter and I hugged him. "We'll see, honey," I said, and we followed Christine into her closet-sized office. "I overheard the nurses talking," Ben said, trailing behind me. "They said my insurance only covers three days in acute care." I recalled Peter remarking that the hospital would probably keep Ben until the insurance ran out, and I wondered if it was purely coincidence that the discussion of his discharge was taking place on the third day.

Christine's office had a plant in the corner. Part of me wondered if she even knew it was there. I looked at Ben. You don't belong in here, kiddo, I thought. I do. I'm becoming more cynical and suspicious by the minute. My attitude sucks.

We all sat there for a few moments with frozen, plastic smiles stuck to our faces. Everyone except Ben. Radiating anxiety, he rubbed his palms against his jeans and scratched the little red bumps all over his arms and legs. Knowing Ben, he was undoubtedly convinced that he'd been singled out for an experiment in germ warfare. I had told him countless times it was just a simple rash — that people get rashes in the winter when they have sensitive skin and the air gets dry. He's driven me crazy worrying about his rash ever since it appeared.

The minute part of my personality I still recognized wanted to hug him hard and overwhelm him with reassurances, but I suspected that if he mentioned the rash now, Christine would know exactly what his problem was because I'd suddenly start yelling, "Please, not the rash. I don't want to hear about your rash. And for God's sake, stop scratching."

Abruptly, Ben broke the silence. "Can I go home today?" he asked.

Christine cleared her throat and we all sat up straight like school children waiting for the teacher's instructions. "That's one of the things we're here to determine," she said. "But perhaps we should start," she said, "with you telling your parents what you've learned during your stay here."

As if rehearsing his part in the school play, he promptly started to recite the life lessons he had accumulated in approximately seventy-two hours. Although I had vowed to pay attention, my mind began to wander. My curiosity was piqued — I'd been his mother for fifteen years, and I still couldn't get him to bring his laundry downstairs in the morning. What could he have possibly learned in less than three days?

I forced myself to listen. He talked about the three-step plan he had been taught to avoid self-injury, to preempt a repeat performance of Friday's nightmare. I nodded my approval, and then something occurred to me. "Has Ben seen his doctor?" I asked.

"The doctor hasn't made his rounds yet," Christine replied. I put my hand over my mouth as if to physically prevent myself from speaking the words rising like bile from the pit that taken up permanent residence in my stomach. How in heaven's name can you consider discharging him when he hasn't even seen his doctor?

"I can phone and see if he's here," she said. "He may have a few minutes to meet with Ben."

She dialed the phone and spoke for a few moments with someone on the other end. Wearing a broad smile, she replaced the receiver and turned to us. "I've got good news," she said. "His doctor's in the building and he's agreed to meet with both you and Ben after we finish here. You're lucky. He doesn't often do this."

I forced myself to smile and provided the requisite nod. Wow, aren't we special, I thought. Add excessive sarcasm to the list of my appealing personality traits. I'd been concerned about talking too much, but as the session continued, I was sickened into silence. I kept seeing Ben standing there in the bathroom, surrounded by blood-soaked towels, his face tortured with terror. I kept hearing him say, "Mom, am I going to die?"

"Do you have something you want to share with us, Mrs. Thomas?" Christine asked.

A thick, uncomfortable silence filled the room as I struggled to extricate something complete and coherent from the tangled mess of thoughts that had rendered me speechless. Finally, I said, "I don't want this to ever happen again. I don't want to lose my son. I don't think I could take it." Way to go, I thought. Now, that was profound. Truly inspired. Christine's expression said, "Well, duh." I tried to explain, but nothing came out the way I wanted it to. Ben's eyes filled with disappointment, and I knew what he was thinking. Help me out here, Mom. I'm trying to go home.

Peter gently interrupted. "We're prepared to do whatever is necessary to help Ben. Of course he's going to need help on an out-patient basis, and we'll do whatever we can to facilitate that." Then he turned to Ben. "I'm going to try a lot harder, too, Ben. I'd rather take a knife and cut my own arm than see you hurt yourself again."

Here we go again, I thought, as tears filled my eyes. Christine scribbled something on her trusty clipboard. She probably wrote, "Mother makes obvious, self-centered statements. Cries all the time."

Mercifully, the phone rang. Christine hung up and

announced that the doctor was ready to see Ben. After Ben disappeared into the doctor's office, Peter and I wandered out into the lounge where several other kids were eating their lunch. I spotted the Styrofoam container marked with Ben's name and opened it. Peter stared at me in amazement as I picked up a fork and began to eat what looked like a pork chop and stuffing. There was limp puddle of green beans and some applesauce. "That's Ben's lunch," he said.

I stopped and looked at the fork on its way to my mouth as if I had no idea how it got there. "Oh God, you're right. I don't know what the hell I'm doing." I closed the container and put it on the table beside me. I wasn't sure that even our dog would've eaten those green beans, and we're talking about a dog that once ate some aluminum foil.

The doctor was studying some papers in front of him when we walked into the office. We waded through the required introductions and hand shaking, the mind-numbing small talk, and the inevitable, expectant silence. I wanted to hear what profound insights the doctor had gained from his ten- minute interview with my son. Another quick glance at his papers and he spoke. "I've decided that Thomas can go home today."

Peter leaned over and peered at the paper in front of the doctor. "Our son's first name is Ben. His last name is Thomas. Someone's made a mistake filling out this form."

The doctor raised his hand, as if dismissing even the smallest possibility of an error. Peter apologized for interrupting, and with a forgiving nod, the doctor continued. "I've decided that your son can return home today. He'll continue with the medication I've prescribed, and I'd like to set up an appointment with him as soon as possible. He'll also need an appointment with one of the counselors that works in my clinic."

"Is he really ready to come home?" I said. Maybe I should have asked if I was ready for Ben to come home. How could I tell this man, staring at me expectantly and tapping his pen on the desk, how frightened I was — for Ben and for me?

"Yes, I believe he is. Both the counselors and I believe he

has had a very productive stay here. He's an extremely bright and sensitive boy, and I'm sure we'll continue to make progress as I treat him."

I know he's bright, I thought. I know he's sensitive. Tell me something I don't already know, you overpaid piece of crap. Oh God, tell me how this happened. Tell me what to do to make sure it never happens again. Can you tell me anything besides the fucking obvious?

The doctor stood up, signaling the end of our interview. Peter shook his hand. "Thank you for taking the time to see us," he said.

Oh, for God's sake, I thought and left.

Ben jumped up from his chair as soon he saw me. "Can I come home?"

I smiled and nodded. "Your dad and I will find out what the deal is for discharge, and we'll spring you from this joint."

"I'm going to go and pack my bag," he said and took off down the hall.

I felt Peter's hand on my shoulder, and I blinked hard, determined not to cry and spoil this for Ben. "I'm scared," I whispered. "I'm so scared."

"Of course you are. I am, too."

"You are?"

"Yeah. I think it's okay to be scared. But not too scared to act, you know?"

"I just want to wrap him up in a blanket or something and keep him in a closet or his room. I guess I'm angry, too. I don't know why, but I'm so damn mad. God, I don't know what to think. Or to do."

"We can do lots of things. Including going to family therapy. I hope you don't mind, but I asked the doctor about it. He thought it was a great idea."

"I bet he did. We can finance his next trip to Europe." Stop it, I thought. Peter's trying, Ben's trying. Get with the program. "I guess I'm not going to stop being frightened overnight, huh?"

"Nope. 'Fraid not. Give it some time, okay? He put his arms around me, holding me gently as though I was the fragile one — the one who had been injured. It was like he understood exactly how I felt, as if he knew that when Ben cut his arm open, he left all three of us bleeding. I closed my eyes for a moment. It felt so good to be held.

When I opened my eyes and stepped away from Peter's arms, I saw Ben walking towards us. His broad smile and confident step didn't fool me for a minute. My precious man-child was frightened, too. "Ready to go?" I asked.

"Yeah, I sure am."

I turned to Peter. "Maybe we should make an appointment for that family thing you mentioned. I mean, while we're here and all."

He shoved his hand into his front pocket and pulled out a small white card. "I thought we could always cancel it later." He shrugged and hesitated for a few seconds. "In case one of us didn't want to go or something."

I took the card from his hand and stared at it. "I think it's a fine idea. Come on guys, let's go home."

We left with Ben in the lead, hurrying as if he worried that the doctor might suddenly change his mind and order him to stay. As we passed the giant fig tree, I noticed a middle-aged woman wth a large pitcher watering the plant. Peter touched my arm. "Look," he said. "Somebody actually noticed the plant."

I smiled and took his arm. "Hey, what do you know? Maybe it'll still be here when we come back."

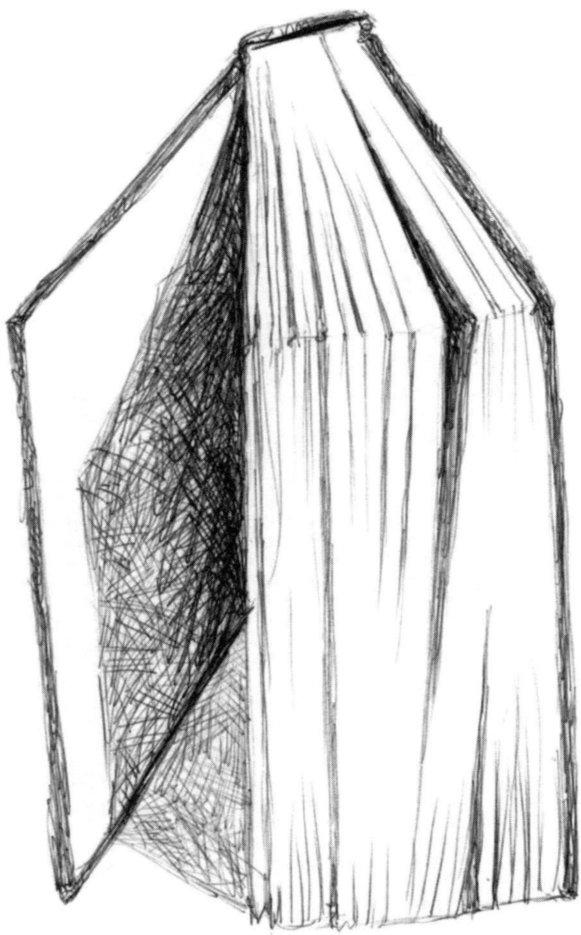

Damon Stewart

[Damon's publicist is out today, so the intern wrote the following:] Damon lives with his wife and two children in Rensselaer, NY. He works for a hospital in New York's Capital Region, and has had stories and articles appear in the *Morpo Review*, *Full Circle Journal*, *American Motorcyclist*, *CC Motorcycle Newsmagazine*, and the *Albany Times-Union*.

likes

(the late, great) Warren Zevon; my motorcycle; Brewery Ommegang; Gus' Hot Dog Stand; Valentine's; Adult Swim on the Cartoon Network; that flash when you see the whole thing come together; Sheryl Crow; my children, wife and family (in varying order, depending on the day); William Gibson; Frankenfiction; calmly moving forward; naps on the front porch when it's sunny out

dislikes

Doing things your way; lack of air conditioning; my inability to change domestic or foreign policy; having to paint the porch (and this spring I have to do it, I can't put it off another year); the loose reins on time; knowing it won't work, trying it anyway and having it not work; the cost of daycare, healthcare and education; moving the clocks forward or back (it always messes me up)

Lost in the Static

The day after I heard that Ray had broken up with Rachael I stopped by his apartment to see if he was ok. He's my older brother, but for a long time I've been the one who looks out for him. I didn't expect him to be a total mess or anything, but still, they had been pretty tight.

I found him in the living room, sitting on the floor by the stereo staring into space. He was holding a pair of black headphones in his lap. He saw me and grunted, then, "Dave, you ever hear of a radio station that's called `Radio for the Land of the Heart'?"

"No."

"What?"

"No," with emphasis.

He sighed, put the headphones back on and hunched over the stereo, fiddling with the dial. I noticed a stack of empty beer cans next to him, a Leaning Tower of Genesee with some smaller administrative beer structures surrounding it.

"Heartland Radio?" I asked. I could see that we would ease into the topic of Rachael: no going there straight away.

"Radio for the Land of the Heart."

"Yeah, whatever. Why are you looking for it?"

"It's... it's just a great station. Gotta find it."

"What's so great about it?" I hoped I kept the annoyance out of my voice. Ray was quick to take offense, even with me. But I wanted to know if he was ok; we could listen to the radio later.

Except for the time with Rachael, work was pretty much his

life. He had been working for a local contractor as a carpenter for the past ten years; he kept the job despite his temper because he was so good. Even if a project was finished and they had moved on to the next, Ray would come back after work to get a cabinet just right; maybe a door wasn't fitted to his satisfaction or the kitchen molding was a little off. Whatever it was, he'd work for free and keep at it 'til it was perfect. We both live in the same small town, Delhi, New York, and he had a reputation as a good worker, temper or no. So even if people avoided him socially, he was still considered a good man to have on the job.

He sat back, lifted the 'phones off his head and took a long pull from his beer. "I heard it the first night with Rachael. I'd asked her out at the Great American, right there in line with three people behind me. I figured for sure she'd heard about me and would say no, but what the hell, right?" — this was a shock, since it was the first time I'd heard that Ray was aware that people thought anything about him — "But she said 'sure.' We went to Pizza Hut, then to the movies, saw 'Fight Club.'"

"That didn't have a `Land of the Heart' radio station in it."

"I know Dave, that was later. But we had such a great time, she was just…" He paused and looked up at me, hands in front of him, palms up.

"Yeah," I said. In some ways we understood each other at a pretty basic level. He was the one who told me to marry Sheila, "She's the one for you man, I never seen you so happy." And he said it like he was looking right into me and could see that she was It. He just knew.

"So on the way back, we went parking." He laughed, then took another swig. "Yeah, like a couple of goddamn kids, about a mile up Federal Hill Road. I pulled the car into some hayfield."

I was surprised again. About the only thing other than work that Ray gave a shit about was his car. It was a 1979 Buick Century, metallic red and big as a house. He bought it for $300, painted it, rebuilt the engine and added chrome wheels. He washed it regularly and fretted about parking it in public places for fear of someone scratching it. The thought of Ray driving that car in a field--he must have been smitten with lust.

"So, you know, we…"

"Yeah," I said, grinning.

"Afterwards we hung out, just lying in the back seat. Radio playing, drank a few beers, burned one, you know. Rachael fell asleep against me and I finished the joint, was sort of zoning, and next thing I know the radio's playing all these great tunes, ones from back when I was a kid."

Well shoot, I thought to myself, he was just stoned and listening to some oldies station.

"And?"

"I listened for about half an hour, then it faded out."

"Faded out?"

"Yeah, just got all static and went away. I tried to get it back, but Rachael woke up and had to get home."

"So let's hear it," and I nodded at the stereo.

"That's just fucking it: I can't find it. I don't remember where it was on the dial. Christ, I don't even know if it was AM or FM. It sounded a little too rough for FM, but I never have it on AM. I don't know; Rach and I were kickin' around in the front seat for awhile, maybe it got switched to AM."

"Yeah, maybe. Listen Ray, I'm just making sure you're, you know… things are cool. Want to come and have dinner with us? Danny and Little Ray have been asking about you. They want to wrestle." Before Rachael, he probably spent more time with my sons than anyone else, they had something together. Almost like the two of us when we were kids.

But he wasn't listening anymore. He had put the headphones back on and cracked another beer. I watched for a minute as he slowly ran the dial up and down the band, then, "Bye Ray."

He didn't answer.

I didn't talk to him for about two weeks after that. Danny, my youngest, got sick and Sheila had some important project to finish at work, so I had to stay home for a few days. The following weekend I had to fix a leaky pipe in the basement, then some catching up to do on my job, then… you know, all that stuff. The older you get the faster time goes, and one day you suddenly realize this isn't just a saying from people older than you.

Then one night, about 3:30 am, the phone rang. It scared the hell out of me and I picked it up with my heart racing. I could feel Sheila sitting up behind me.

"Hello?"

"Hey man, it's me. You got a radio there?"

"What?"

"You got a radio there?"

"Ray?"

There was a silence, as both of us processed the state of mind of the other. He started again, this time slowly.

"Is-there-a-radio-there?"

"Ray, what is—" But I realized that this needed to be continued somewhere else. I turned around and addressed the figure in the darkness — "It's ok, it's just Ray. I think he's been drinking."

Sheila settled back under the covers with an annoyed sigh and I took the cordless downstairs, out to the front porch.

"Ray, what's going on? Where are you? Is everything ok? Have you been—"

"DAVE! Just get to a radio! Please!"

That scared me more than the phone, the pleading tone in his voice. Never in my life did I imagine I'd hear my brother beg for anything, and sure as fucking hell not with that sound in his voice.

I ran into the kitchen where we had one of those clock-radios screwed underneath a cabinet.

"Ok Ray, I'm at a radio."

"Turn it on, AM, 1320."

I did, but all I got was static. "Ray, there's nothing but noise."

"Listen carefully."

I leaned my head close to the radio, my ear almost touching

the speaker. The hiss was punctuated only by sharp crackles and pops. Then, just for a moment, something came through, barely. I think I heard music. It was possible anyway.

"I'm not sure Ray, maybe something for a second there, but—"

"You don't hear it?"

"Hear what?"

He mumbled something, then, "Try this." Suddenly a blast of white noise made me pull the phone away from my ear. It lasted for about ten seconds, then, "Dave, did you hear it?

"All I heard was static. What's going on?"

"I think I found it. I think Radio for the Land of the Heart is at AM 1320."

"Ok." I had that neutral tone just perfect.

"Yeah, I know there's some noise, but if you listen real careful, you can hear the tune. I think that was `Dancing in the Moonlight.' Man, I love that song."

"Ray."

"Um?"

"Ray, you ok? Have you been drinking?"

"No, I just thought I found the goddamn radio station Dave; I thought fucking maybe you'd want to hear it."

"Ray, I just—"

"Fuck you, bro, when I find it I won't tell you. Then it'll be your tough shit."

It happened at least four more times over the next couple weeks: Ray would call and say that he found the station, put the phone up to his stereo speaker and explain what song could be teased out of the hiss. I never actually heard any of it, but he believed he heard something. It didn't matter though. Sooner or later, whether by finally hearing the station identification or realizing that it was just noise, Ray would conclude that it wasn't "Land of the Heart" radio and try again.

He must have been trying a little too hard. I was in the Great American one night after work, buying some ketchup so the boys wouldn't set up a howl at dinner. Bottle of Heinz in hand, I was walking towards the checkout when I ran into Ray's boss, Sandy.

"Hey Sandy, what's up?" He was holding two large bags full of groceries and heading for the door, but when he saw me he stopped, put the bags on a nearby bench and turned to me with a serious look.

"Dave, you've got to talk to your brother."

"Hmm?" I've heard this before. Many times, actually. Usually the person I'm talking to goes on to tell me how they saw Ray the night before at the Shire or Anthony's Attic or some other bar, how Ray started out in a good mood, "but he was just throwing back those drinks, shots, beer, Christ Dave, he can down 'em," or something to that effect. I just nod and let them get on with it. Then they follow up with, "all of the sudden he got mad." Then the story devolves into how Ray, "went right after me Dave, and all I said was that he spilled something on his shirt," or "he tried to take on the whole bar Dave, I swear he wanted to fight five guys, and they weren't small guys, either…" sort of thing. No one is mad at me, not usually. All the locals understand that I have no control over him, but they always fill me in on the latest.

But it wasn't anything like that. Sandy just said, "Ray hasn't shown up for work in two weeks. 'Cept to pick up his check, last Thursday."

"Shoot, Sandy, I don't know what's going on. I haven't seen him in awhile; Sheila and I have been real busy lately and—"

"I was there when he came into the office to get his check, Dave. He looked like hell. Pale, skinnier than usual, hadn't taken a shower in awhile." Sandy glanced around, then took a step closer. "I think you need to get him some help. Rehab maybe. He's on something."

I looked out the window.

"I haven't fired him yet. I can't do that; he's a fuc— He's a character, Dave, but I like the guy. He's one of the best I got." Sandy put his hand on my shoulder. "Listen, you get him in a program somewhere and you let me know. I'll do what I can to help you out. Your brother's a good man, we need him around."

I don't know if I ever heard anyone say that before. The measure of Sandy's decency wasn't just what he said, but also the fact that he walked away, pretending to check his watch while I pretended to scratch something around my eye.

Dinner was waiting, but instead of heading home I drove over to Ray's apartment on Main Street, above Dubben's Hardware store. Walking up the staircase, I remember this particular feeling of dread, one that I always associate with Ray. It's hard to explain, but for years now, late at night or sometimes when I am focused on a job or fixing something in the basement, suddenly Ray will pop into my head and I'll be worried about him. No particular reason, but it's like there's this hole in my heart, empty, just waiting to be lined with a pain that I've yet to discover. And it's got something to do with Ray. I'll feel bad, for him and for me. Like I have just an inkling of his sorrow, and there's nothing I can do about it.

He was inside. The place wasn't clean, but it wasn't any worse by Ray standards. He was lying on the couch, face pale, dark circles under his eyes. But I wasn't thinking drugs or drinking. I mean, he's my brother, and I could always tell when the guy wasn't straight. Although I wasn't exactly relieved either: it was clear that he hadn't slept in awhile. A long while. But before I could ask him what was going on with Sandy, he launched right into it.

"Dave, listen, did you know that radio waves can bounce off the atmosphere? Especially AM waves; they can travel halfway across the country if conditions are right."

"Huh. Anyway, how you feeling? You look a little tired."

"So I'm thinking that "Land of the Heart" radio is coming from the Midwest. Makes sense, y'know? `Heartland' and all that. I'm only getting it late at night when the conditions are right." He saw the look on my face. "It's not me Dave, it's true, there's lots of AM stations you can only get at night. Listen."

He got up and walked over to the stereo. It was already on and he turned up the volume, the speakers discharging a familiar scraping noise. "It's just crap now, but around midnight-one, that's a classical music station out of Binghamton. That must be what, 50, 70 miles from here? And this—" a twist of the dial, more of the same noise—"this is a heavy metal station, I'm pretty sure it's from Philly. You gotta wait until at least 2:00 AM to hear it. Heavy metal on AM radio. That's weird."

"Right. Ray, I ran into Sandy today and—"

"Yeah, yeah, where have I been." He turned the stereo off. "I got some vacation time coming. He'll just charge it against that."

"Yeah but Ray, why?"

"Why what?"

"Why aren't you working?"

He looked at me as if I'd asked him whether he considered breathing important to daily living.

"You wouldn't get it." He turned back to the stereo, switching it back on and peering intently at the dial.

"C'mon Ray— what's going on?"

"I have to find that station. I know it's taking a lot of time but I only need a few more days. I've been keeping this chart—" He reached behind the stereo and pulled out a pad of lined yellow paper, thick with blue ink, a handmade grid covering the entire page and tiny handwriting filling each block— "I've been pretty methodical about it. I'm keeping this chart so I don't keep finding the same stations. Whenever I get something I listen to it for a while, make sure that's not it, then move on to the next one. I'm keeping track of both AM and FM.

"All that just to find a radio station? You just go up and down the dial, right?"

"It's not that easy. At night you might get two different stations on the same spot, depending on the time. 'Specially on AM. They fade in and out, so you have to keep the dial in one place for hours just to be sure. Like here, 590?" He turned and pointed at the stereo, near the lower end of the dial, "Last night I got two different stations. WBZX during the day, plays oldies. They sign off at midnight, then I get this country station out of Wilkes-Barre. Around four in the morning WBZX starts up again."

Well, I thought to myself, that explained the lack of sleep.

"Hey," and he suddenly turned to me. "I've been meaning to ask — can you check the internet? The fucker might be on there, right? Look for—"

"—Radio for the Land of the Heart. Got it. Will do."

"Thanks, Dave," and I saw a smile crack his face. It was a little scary, like he was trying to be gracious. Ray did not have a computer. Ray didn't give a damn about the internet. Ray was not gracious. Things were getting strange, and I should have had a clue right then and there what was coming.

"This is taking longer than I thought, you know?" he continued, scratching the stubble on his jaw and looking again at the chart. "'Course, as soon as I find that station…"

I waited for him to finish the sentence, but he just stared down at the stereo. After a few moments of silence I said goodbye and walked out, split between relief and worry. Relief, because Ray wasn't doing drugs or drinking (I mean Drinking; everything is relative). He was going through the standard girlfriend crisis, I told myself, just trying to deal with Rachael leaving. Maybe he thought the station would bring back memories or something. But eventually he'd find the station, nothing would happen, and he'd get over it.

Probably. That was the worry part.

So I tried to help; after dinner I spent an hour on the `net googling "Radio for Land of the Heart," "radio," "1320," "590" and so on. I tried every combination I could think of, but no luck. No radio station, that is. "Land of the Heart" got me 337 hits, including a Mother's Day site, three travel agencies, a fantasy novel and several Christian-related links. But no radio station.

That night, in bed, I told Sheila about it. She said that I should spend some time with him, "invite him over for dinner, see if he wants to spend the night." That's when I knew it sounded bad to her too, because she never offered to have him stay over. Whenever he'd visit and dinner was through or the when video ended, she'd wish him a good night and a safe ride home, the hint clear, regardless of weather or late hour.

I went over to his place the next day after work. He was sleeping on the living room floor, headphones on, a faint hiss coming from them. I shook him awake, waited for him to stagger back from the bathroom, and asked him over for supper.

"Nah, I got to keep looking," and he jerked his elbow towards the stereo.

The whole radio thing was getting to be a bit much, so I figured it was as good a time as any to bring up the other subject. "Seen Rachael lately?"

"She called me the other day. Wanted to go out."

I waited as Ray began picking up the empty beer cans and food wrappers scattered throughout the room.

"And?"

He walked into the kitchen, his arms full of greasy paper and dripping aluminum. I heard the muffled crunch of the mess getting wedged into his overflowing wastebasket, and he walked back into the room.

"And what? I said no. It wasn't working out. She's nice, but… I dunno. Kept trying to tell me what to do."

"But, I thought you really liked her, I mean—"

"I do, Dave. We're still friends. I'm going to meet her for coffee the day after tomorrow."

"Then I don't get it. Why is it you want to find that radio station? I mean, I thought it had something to do with Rachael, getting her back, that sort of thing."

"Well, shit, even if I wanted her back, what does the radio station have to do with it?"

"Well Christ, what is it about that station, then? You're way too into this, man. I'm getting, you know, kinda worried."

He grimaced and turned his back to me, looking out the window at the streetlight illuminating the empty Main Street. "I don't know if I can explain it, Dave. There's just something about it, those songs the DJ was playing. It brought it all back. Like when I was a kid; those summers I used to hang out at Jim Coffey's house. We'd sit around on his front porch and watch the cars go by, just shooting the breeze. He'd play his brother's records and we'd spend all afternoon there; me, Jim, Ed Leno and Janice Stratton. Remember her? I had such a crush on her. Damn. Those were the days, man. Before things got all… you know. I know I've — it was like the good times coming back over the radio. Yeah."

He was silent for a moment; I thought he'd forgotten about me and was about to clear my throat when he continued.

"It's not that big a deal, really. I just want to listen to that station, see if they play more songs from those days. Get that feeling back. Maybe I can figure out how I'm going to…" He shook his head then turned back around to face me. "Want a beer?"

I wish I had gotten him to finish that sentence. I don't know what he was going to say, but now I think it might have helped me find a way to reach in and bring him back from wherever he'd gone for the past decade or so. But I just let it go. "No thanks. When are you going back to work?"

"Next Monday. I spoke to Sandy this afternoon, everything's cool. He needs me back and Sandy's a good guy anyway."

Walking out the door, I told myself that maybe the whole Rachael episode was good for Ray. "Sandy's a good guy" and "I'm going to meet her for coffee" were just the sort of nice, well-adjusted things we'd all been hoping for years that he would start saying. When I told Sheila, she said, "Maybe Ray's starting to figure out his priorities in life. Maybe he just needs a friend right now, they did seem to get along. He's a good man, Dave, he just needs to settle down and focus. Let's try again; invite him over in a week."

The next several days flew by with no word from him. I work for the county paper, a weekly, doing some graphic design, a little editing, a little sales, whatever needs to be done between me, three other employees and the owner. It pays well enough and I can lose myself in the job, trying to make the deadline and no mistakes, and everyone I work with is pretty calm under pressure. So I managed to forget about Ray for awhile, until one evening when Sheila reminded me to call him.

Ray didn't answer the phone, but sometimes he just ignores it so I had to go check in person. Pulling into his driveway, it took about two seconds to figure out he wasn't there. Car gone, lights out, mail piled up outside his door. I went back and told Sheila.

"Maybe he's visiting some old friends. Maybe he went on vacation. After all Dave, it's not like he has to check in with you."

But she didn't believe any of it either.

The next night, 12:15 a.m., the phone rang. I felt a twinge of fear. Thinking of Ray and his car crumpled around a tree. Flames.

"Dave."

"Ray, man, where are you?"

"Missouri; a few miles north of Joplin. Rt. 71 I think."

"Jesus Christ Ray, what the fuck are you doing in Missouri?" I could feel Sheila sitting up behind me. "Missouri?" I heard her ask.

"Still trying to find Radio for the Land of the Heart, Dave." Then I noticed how tired he sounded. And something else, not quite like he was drunk, but there was an odd quality to his voice, a strain.

"Ray, listen to me, why don't you get to a motel and sit tight. I can—" I had to think; driving would take a couple of days, no way he'd be able to sit still for that long. We'd just about paid the credit card off, but — "I'll get a plane to the nearest city and come and get you. We'll fly back and—"

"Dave, I don't need anyone to come and get me. That station's got to be around here somewhere."

"Ray—" I whispered through clenched teeth, "You got to—"

"Ahh shit Dave," his voice got tight, like he was starting to cry, "I been looking for a week now, and I just can't find it. It's got to be here somewhere. Got to be."

"Ray, why didn't you tell me you were going to take off and go looking for it?"

"What the fuck were you gonna do? You think I'm crazy like everyone else. Screw you all. I have to find that station. I figured if I drove out here I'd find it. I mean it reached all the way to goddamn

Delhi, Dave. It's got to be some huge station. I haven't heard it yet, but I will. And when I do, I'm going to find that DJ, sit in the booth with him and drink a beer and listen to the old days."

"Ray, please—"

A mechanical voice interrupted, informing us that Ray had to add two dollars within the next thirty seconds.

"Ray, listen, you got to stay there, I'll help you find the station, I'll—"

"Thanks Dave." He sounded different now, like he had stopped crying and suddenly cheered up. "I'll be alright. I got some cash saved up, it's not like I been living high on the hog, know what I mean?" He laughed.

"Ray, please, man, please—"

"20 seconds," said the voice.

"Ray, call me back collect."

"OK, I'll talk to you later."

I sat there for about half an hour waiting for him to call. Eventually Sheila said, "I don't think he's calling back David," and gave me a hug. "Can you sleep? Want me to get you anything?"

I couldn't sleep and she couldn't get me anything, so I went downstairs and turned on the TV. There was nothing on so I walked out on the front porch and sat on the couch for a while. It was one of those hot, humid summer nights, the kind where you'd better have air-conditioning or little need for sleep. We had AC in our bedroom, as did the kids, but the rest of the place was a sauna. I walked back into the house, crept upstairs and grabbed my jeans and a t-shirt. On my way out, Sheila said, "Where are you going?"

"For a walk."

"Don't do anything… silly Dave. Please."

"Don't worry."

I stopped at the top of the stairs to open the door and peek into the boys' room — Danny and Ray were sound asleep. Danny was clutching a plastic fire truck; little Ray was sprawled on the floor, his sheet wrapped around his body and neck. I unwrapped the sheet and put him back in bed. I gave them both a kiss, went downstairs to put on my clothes, and walked out.

The Shire Pub was only two blocks away from the house. It was almost empty, just the bartender and a lone customer, watching a "Star Trek" re-run. I got a seat with a good view of the T.V., ordered a cold one, then another, and by the time I left I had managed to make myself tired.

I floated through the next day, worried and hung over, trying to figure out what to do. That night, tired as I was, I still couldn't sleep, wondering if I should call the police, maybe try to find some sort of help line that Ray could call, something, anything. When I finally dozed off, it wasn't for long; the phone rang around 3:30am.

"Dave!" He sounded positively joyful.

"Where are you?"

"Um… Guthrie, Oklahoma. I think. Least that's what the sign at the liquor store says. Listen, I got time on a phone card, so we have a few minutes."

Oh Jesus, I thought, he's getting further away. "Ray, please, please listen to me. Why can't you just wait and let me come out there? I'll help you find that station."

"That's why I called, man! I found the fucker! Hold on!" The phone clanked down and a moment later I heard the clack and groan of a car door opening, then a blast of static, a faint beat just noticeable. He grabbed the phone again. "You hear it? Hear it Dave? Dave?"

"Maybe something. It's kind of rough though."

"Wait a minute," he said, and the phone smacked down again, dangling I assumed, by the cord in some godforsaken phone booth in Guthrie, Oklahoma.

He must have adjusted the dial, because it got clearer. There was a DJ talking, listing the last few songs that had been played, all of them sounding vaguely familiar, although I couldn't specifically recall any of the tunes. Then he started playing "Waterloo Sunset" by the Kinks, a song I swear I haven't heard since I was a teenager.

And it hit me. Like the way I think it must have hit Ray: the music brought back these memories, not of anything in particular, but a collage of those days when we were kids and everyone listened to AM radio. Long hours on the road during a family vacation and the miles passing by. Man-made beaches on Adirondack lakes, the thin layer of sand giving way to dirt in two plastic shovelfuls. Small amusement parks, the worn-out rides creaking their burden to screams and laughter. Gas stations illuminated by neon lights. Sitting in a diner, the sun blinding me through a window, ordering pancakes. I saw myself playing kick-the-can out behind the school, Ray running ahead of me and laughing. Then I'm throwing snowballs at cars. Dusk in winter, the cold, and the stillness-

"Dave? What's going on? Is Ray all right?" Sheila asked, jerking me out of it.

"Yeah, hold on," and I held up a finger.

The song ended, and the static increased again. I could barely hear the DJ, "This is radio… at… 'teen twenty, the music for the… of the Heart".

Ray was right.

"See? See?" Ray demanded. "It's around here somewhere, it's gotta be. I'm close Dave, might to take me a day or two, but I'll track it down."

"Ray, that station could be anywhere. You heard it out here, remember?"

"Yeah right. Still. I must be getting close. Listen, I got to go. Station's fading, I got to drive around 'til it picks up again. Hang in there kid, say hi to Sheila and the boys, and I'll call you from the station." He laughed, then, "Hey, maybe I'll get the DJ to dedicate a song to you-how about "Kung Fu Fighting? You used to dance around to that song, it was a riot. You were so serious."

"Ray, I can be out there in-"

"OK buddy, gotta go. Later."

"Ray wait!" I yelled as it hit me, the one thing he didn't say. "Where is it on the dial?"

But he hung up.

The next day I called the FCC — they never heard of it. I

went back on the 'net and got the phone numbers for a bunch of radio stations in Oklahoma. But I only heard the same, "Radio what?" I called surrounding states, places selected at random, cities and college towns in Kansas, Arkansas, Texas. No luck. But the Midwest is huge, right? I couldn't call every city, every town; I couldn't cover them all. It could be some desolate, on-the-edge-of-nowhere plains radio, their "Best of the '70's" hour-long special every third Tuesday of the month, and how would I find it?

A friend told me about pirate radio — guys who will set up their own station out of their garage. He'd even heard about these operations that set up on boats sailing up and down the Mississippi, trying to keep one step ahead of the FCC. But he doubted any pirate radio in the Midwest, even under the best conditions, would get as far as New York. But who knows? Ray definitely found something.

That was all about three weeks ago. I haven't heard from him since.

I stayed up every night since that last phone call, crouched by the radio in the living room, trying to find the station. I went to Ray's apartment to get his chart, so I could pick up where he left off, but he must have taken it with him.

Last week I started staying home; I needed to catch up on my sleep. Sheila didn't say anything, even though I was burning up vacation time that we had planned to use on a trip to the Finger Lakes. I could tell she was getting worried about me, though.

A few days ago I bought a bunch of maps of the Midwest, trying to figure out where Ray had been, where he might be going. He was methodical by nature; he must have had some system for driving around and looking. I was just guessing of course, but I had some ideas on how he might do it; he's my brother after all.

It was Sheila's folks, Bud and Stacey, who got the show on the road, so to speak. Three days ago they stopped by after dinner and offered me money, "to help you find him." Stacey said, "To be honest, David, I don't approve of him, but family is family," and I thanked Bud as he handed over a wad of cash. I knew they were thinking private detective, but I also knew there was only one way to do this. The next morning, after Sheila left with the kids for school and work, I took off.

So here I am — driving north on the Interstate, heading out of Oklahoma into Kansas. My right arm is sore from holding it out and turning the radio dial all day.

Guthrie consisted of a post office, about a dozen houses, a general store, a diner and a liquor store. It took all of five minutes to learn from a waitress at the diner that Ray had been there (it's that small; they remember the strangers). He had left the same night he called me after asking for directions to I-35.

I think I know what Ray was trying to find. It's like that rapid, scurrying movement at twilight that you see out of the corner of your eye when you're a kid. You turn to chase it and it's gone — but you know something was there. You stop seeing it when things like girls, the price of gas, new appliances, become important. Or maybe you make yourself stop seeing it. But I remember, back then, thinking that if I could only follow that thing, it would lead me to some secret passageway, a hidden door at the back of my parent's closet or the entrance to a small cave, covered by the bushes out behind the barn. And if you could get through the door or inside the cave, you'd find… I don't know. Another world I guess; like those stories your folks read to you when you were little and they seemed real as anything else. Back then I could just feel it out there, lurking on the edge of perception. Listening to that station, I got that feeling again, only stronger, like it crawled out of that cave and grabbed me by the throat.

I have a plan. I know the station exists, and Ray's right, it's probably in the Midwest. And he knows it exists, of course, and like the saying goes, he may be crazy but he's not stupid. He'll find it eventually, and he'll drink that beer with the DJ. You could just tell by the DJ's voice that he was the kind of guy who'd let visitors hang out.

So if I find that station, I find my brother. If I find it first, I'll just wait for him. The kids can come out with their mother and stay with me until he shows up. Either way, I'll get him, take him home, and make him better. Or try to, anyway.

The exit is coming up, just a few miles to go and I'm in Wichita. The teenage waitress in Guthrie told me that there was a public radio station there that "plays really old stuff."

Dennis Dillingham

Dennis Dillingham earned a Bachelor of Arts degree in English with honors from the College of the Holy Cross in Worcester, Massachusetts. His publishing history includes the short story "The White Carousel Horse", which was selected as a finalist for the MTV - Pocket Books Short Story Contest for Young Writers. The story subsequently appeared in the book *Pieces - A Collection of New Voices*, edited by Stephen Chbosky (author of *Perks of Being a Wallflower*) and published by Pocket Books in Aug. 2000.

Dennis currently works as a Copywriter for Weber Shandwick Worldwide in New York City, one of the world's leading public relations firms. A long-time resident of New Jersey, Dennis currently lives in Hoboken. According to uncorroborated sources, he knows all the words to Copa-Cobana and once chugged a bottle of ketchup for money.

likes

People that are nice to me, medium-rare bacon cheddar burgers, drinking beer in the afternoon, drinking beer in the evening, occasionally drinking beer in the morning to offset the effects of having drank too much beer the previous afternoon and evening, short naps, long naps, Kurt Vonnegut, cartoons, dogs that stick their heads out car windows, coffee in all its glorious manifestations, America's Funniest Home Videos, Bruce Springsteen, the Counting Crows, the McRib Sandwich (may it rest in peace), diets that tell me I can lose weight by eating steak topped with bacon dripping in cheese

dislikes

People that are mean to me, Dr. Phil (has our cultural fabric truly disintegrated to the point that so many will blindly accept advice from a balding, mustached Tony Robbins wannabe?), pigeons, Dutch beer, people in Jeeps who wave to other people in Jeeps, Whoopi Goldberg (what dirt does she have on Hollywood anyway?), people who don't think the movie *Best in Show* is funny, the Jake years on California Dreams, Sallie Mae, war, famine, pillaging, destruction, yadda, yadda, yadda…

Two Octogenarians Sitting at a Starbucks Drinking Orange Juice

Two octogenarians sitting at a Starbucks drinking orange juice at 6:00 p.m. on a Tuesday. It sounds like the start to a bad poem, doesn't it? Or maybe a good one, something Wallace Stevens or William Carlos Williams might pen, embracing the seemingly most mundane objects or visions as the truest representations of beauty our world can offer. I don't know. I could never tell the difference between good poetry and bad, outside of the rhyming patterns, which I was told later was no way to judge a poem, no way at all, and I should be ashamed of myself for thinking a poem's worth was tied directly to the pleasure it brought to the ear, ignoring, as it were, the pleasure it brought to the intellect. But, in any case, there they were, sipping away on two twelve ounce bottles of Tropicana 100% orange juice, talking like two people might at Starbucks, having what was most likely an entirely normal and innocent conversation, perhaps about the failing state of the Social Security system or their grandchildren, all entirely normal and expected, except, of course, for the orange juice. I was on my way to her house when I saw them, passing by the same wide pane of logo mottled glass I had passed hundreds of times before, maybe thousands.

Two eighty-something-year-old men sitting at Starbucks, *Starbucks*, sharing orange juice, *orange juice*. It isn't a strange sight, I guess, especially in a city like this, where strangeness is the norm, the only constant, isn't out of the ordinary to see two people drinking orange juice. It's a common beverage, but to be drinking it at Starbucks, to be drinking it at 6:00 p.m. on a Tuesday in early June. Tell me this isn't strange.

She let me in when I got there, still, after all this time, compelled to buzz from the lobby and even knock on her apartment door when I reached the fourth floor, never quite comfortable using the key she had insisted I take. We hugged and kissed and I thought about how it used to be with us, how a situation like this would lead immediately to sex, how no moment alone, regardless of where or when, would go by without the two of us punctuating it with a rousing roll in the hay. She probably thought about it too, the difference between us now and then. *Now and Then. That was then this is now.* What ominous phrases those are, portents of an approaching storm, imminent change. We didn't have sex. We simply said hello and hugged and kissed and headed out for the night.

I didn't tell her about the orange juice or the two old men drinking it, but the whole night I couldn't keep from wondering what they were talking about and how it came to be that they both had a craving for orange juice at 6:00 p.m. on a Tuesday in early June, and had decided, of all the places in New York one could likely get a tall, delicious, refreshing glass of orange juice, all the delis and specialty shops, organic and whole food stores, that advertise freshly squeezed juices and juice-based beverages, on Starbucks. She asked me what was bothering me and I told her that it was nothing. It was nothing, wasn't it? Two men drinking orange juice, that's about as nothing as you get without it actually being nothing, which it never really is. "Nothing" doesn't exist outside of maybe the wallet, certainly the bedroom; it's always something everyplace else, always something except in those two places, nothing's only two sanctuaries. She didn't believe me. There was a distance to my thoughts that night and she could sense it. We had been together too long for her not to be able to sense the distractions running interference in my mind like static in a phone line, like a swarm of flies on a television screen. I would have been disappointed if she didn't notice, I really would have been. I mean three years is a long time to be with someone. If after three years you can't tell that someone's thinking about something, be it two old men drinking orange juice in a Starbucks at 6:00 p.m. on a Tuesday or the ever-growing obesity of pigeons or something else entirely, then there's something wrong, there's something that should be done.

She asked and I said "nothing," and she said that she wished that I would tell her. I said that I would tell her if there was anything to tell, but that in this case, at this present moment, in this present situation being discussed right here and now, there was nothing, nothing at all; and I said that, I said that word "nothing" without even a hint of guilt or worry seeping into my thoughts because I didn't feel as if I was lying. I really didn't. She disagreed. I assured her that I was being truthful, honest, forthright, a stand-up guy, a peddler of nothing but the straight and narrow, keeping it all as the crow flies, and she turned away, upset, whimpering about us growing apart and our inability to communicate. I considered then telling her about the two old men and the orange juice, but it just seemed too ridiculous, at that point seemed like another all-too-contrived excuse and I couldn't bring myself to do it. I remained silent and looked at her the way I probably looked at the two old men, wonderingly, my eyes directed as much inward as out.

She asked me if I thought so too, if I thought that we were growing apart, a chasm stretching between us that had, as of late, grown to nearly insurmountable width. I told her I didn't know, that I didn't think so, that I thought things were exactly the same that night as they had been when we met, drunk and sweaty and hungry for anything that could pass for love, settling for lust, that night in the bathroom at Sutton Place three years and five months before. That, it turned out, was the wrong thing to say.

Later, after drinks and more talking, more silence, she said she didn't want to break up, that she felt — she chose her words carefully here, drowning her failing vocabulary, her lack of mental clarity, buttressing her anxiety, her fear, under swell after swell of Amstel Light, buying time — almost obligated to stay with me, especially so soon after my father's death. (He had died the month before of a rare form of blood cancer the cause of which no doctors were ever really able to explain to any level of satisfaction, confident, it seemed, of only one aspect of his condition: his death.) She said she didn't want to abandon me. That too was the wrong thing to say.

Right or wrong though there it was, the cat was out of the bag, the contents of Pandora's box dumped and spread out on the sidewalk for the world to see. The booze, the night, the argument, the years, I guess, the prodigious exasperation with it all, with me, with the situation, yanked it out of her; and I wondered how long it had been festering, when exactly we stopped being a real couple, two people who enjoyed each other's company, who felt woefully incomplete without the other, who, on an emotional and physical level, needed each other, and had merely devolved into two people shackled together by circumstance, one by fear the other by guilt, neither strong enough to call it what it was and run.

That was the beginning of it, the beginning of the end for us. How can you come back from something like that? And to be honest, the beginning of the end was quite close to the end of the end because we wound up ending it later that very same night over a handful of half priced beers at Kate Kearney's, needing booze all the way through our time together: the night we met, the night we first slept together, the night I told her I loved her, the night she said it back, and, finally, that night, the night we would throw everything into the incinerator, cast off the weights and the shadows and the collected mental and emotional debris of the past three years and ostensibly set out toward the horizon of the rest of our lives. What cowards we were.

When I told Charlie about it the next day, he didn't have much to say except to agree with me that is *was* out of the ordinary to see two old men drinking orange juice at Starbucks at 6:00 p.m. on a Tuesday, and neglected to mention what most people would have considered the true point to the story, the cap on the iceberg, the tragedy, that Sharon and I had broken up after willfully investing three years of our mid-twenties in solely each other, tempting the fates, refusing to diversify. That was something Charlie and I shared, in addition to a hole-in-the-wall two bedroom, cockroach colony on East 92nd Street: a unique ability to distill the sole pebble of relevance from a mountain of fluff, a molecule of significance from an ocean of drivel.

It was a sign, wasn't it, the two men and their orange juice? In a place so entirely devoid of things such as signs, so thoroughly barren, scorched free of any notion of depth or meaning or connection to higher planes of anything, consciousness, emotion, love, existing so exclusively on the surface; in a place lacking anything that can be taken or even misconstrued as divine or mystical influence, who's to say seeing something like that, something like two old men drinking orange juice at a Starbucks as a sign is wrong? Look what happened. Look at the changes that were wrought in their wake.

I've walked by the same Starbucks a number of times since that night, even though it's out of the way from everywhere, except, of course, her apartment, which I don't go to anymore, where I've heard some musician named Alister goes now, a Brit, a bassist in some funk-jazz-soul fusion band that plays down in the East Village and who are on the verge of being signed by a major label, they've told me, the people that feel as if I would want to know that sort of information, have some sort of right to it, to see if I can catch another glimpse of the two aging orange juice drinkers. They haven't been there. I haven't seen them since that night.

If I do see them again, I think I will approach them. I'm not just saying that either, it's not one of those "I'm going to do this or that" proclamations that lose all poignancy or vigor the moment they leave your mouth. I will. I have to. I will ask them what they are doing there at Starbucks not drinking coffee, or at least tea (old men like tea don't they?), but drinking orange juice at a place not at all known for it at a time of day not at all appropriate for juice.

Pasha Malla

"Pasha Malla is a big nerd."
--Aaron Burch

likes	dislikes
The interlocking high-five	The soul-shake

Three Penises of Adelaide, South Australia

Mr. Aberlour

> *"For the phallo-logocentric sublation is with us, and it's militant, regenerating the old patterns, anchored in the dogma of castration."*
>
> - Hélène Cixous, "The Laugh of the Medusa"

There lived in the Bedford Park area of Adelaide a Mr. Clancy Aberlour, whose penis measured three and one-half inches flaccid, five and one-third inches erect. At birth Mr. Aberlour's parents opted to leave him uncircumcised. His foreskin hung limply off the end of his penis like a mitten. As a young boy he was known to his friends as "The Aardvark."

But that was years ago. Mr. Aberlour had since graduated high school, lost his virginity, finished a degree in economics, begun a career, married, and produced one son, Godfrey, whose foreskin was also left unscathed at birth. Mrs. Aberlour expressed indifference to this decision, but Mr. Aberlour saw it as a familial rite of passage.

At eighteen Godfrey moved to Melbourne to pursue a career in the theatre, or at least, acting. Mr. Aberlour was employed by a bank and spent an inordinate amount of time standing with his hand on the Xerox machine, enjoying its warmth as it spewed out copies into a gray plastic tray.

Recently, Mr. Aberlour was experiencing problems with his uncircumcised penis. It seemed his foreskin was tightening, which made it increasingly difficult to clean. He mentioned this dilemma to his wife, who could only express bewilderment

"Whaddya mean, you can't *clean* it?"

"I-I-I can't get the skin back to clean it," stammered Mr. Aberlour.

"Better get that looked at," said Mrs. Aberlour, whose bosom bore an uncanny resemblance to a shelf.

Mr. Aberlour took his penis to the family doctor, a man named Glenn Millinger, who had a grey moustache and the delicate hands of a woman.

"My foreskin won't go back," Mr. Aberlour told Dr. Glenn Millinger.

"Hmm," said the doctor. He was well aware of Mr. Aberlour's penis, having been the man's physician for some thirty-odd years. "Let's have a look at it."

Mr. Aberlour slid his pants down to his ankles and lay down on the vinyl bed in Dr. Glenn Millinger's office. Mr. Aberlour's penis flopped against his thigh, and lay there like a slug. Dr. Glenn Millinger hovered, indecisive, and then lunged forward. He seized the penis between his feminine fingers and had a go at pushing the foreskin back.

"Won't budge, mate," said Dr. Glenn Millinger.

"No," said Mr. Aberlour, grimly.

The doctor stepped back. He went over to a little sink in the corner of his office. Mr. Aberlour pulled up his trousers and sat up on the bed.

"Any pain?" asked Dr. Glenn Millinger over his shoulder, washing his hands.

"No," said Mr. Aberlour. "None yet."

"Burning during urination? Any discomfort? Blood? Foul odour?"

"No, nothing like that. Though," added Mr. Aberlour, "sometimes there's a bit of a *smell* off it."

"Hmm."

The doctor dried his hands on a towel and turned around. "Well, surgery is an option."

"Surgery."

"Sure — it's more common for men than you'd think."

"So, you're talking *circumcision*," Mr. Aberlour whispered.

"I'll give you the number of a specialist." Dr. Glenn Millinger hunched over his desk and wrote something on a notepad. "Dr. Persaud. Indian fellow. Urology clinic up at Flinders."

The doctor straightened up and handed the piece of paper to Mr. Aberlour.

"Right, then," said Mr. Aberlour.

Three weeks later, Mr. Aberlour was scheduled for surgery, an outpatient procedure. Mr. Aberlour would come in the morning, have his foreskin lopped off, take some time to recover, and be out to catch the Crows on the telly that evening. The Indian doctor had reassured Mr. Aberlour it would all be relatively painless. Dr. Persaud's accent gave him an air of dignity that Mr. Aberlour found reassuring.

The day of the operation Mrs. Aberlour sat with her husband while he lay waiting on a cot in a pale green hospital room. The night before Mr. Aberlour had stood naked in front of his bathroom mirror and taken one good long last look at his foreskin. He eventually climbed into bed, where it took ages for him to fall asleep. When he did sleep, he had a peculiar dream with nautical themes.

Sitting in the hospital room, Mrs. Aberlour read aloud bits from a travel magazine to her husband.

"Oh, look at *this*," she would say. "In Japan they've got computerized toilets."

Mr. Aberlour's thoughts were elsewhere.

Finally a pretty nurse came into the room to collect Mr. Aberlour. Mrs. Aberlour called, “Best of luck, love,” as her husband was wheeled out the door, and then promptly returned to an article about the Swedish Archipelago.

In the operating room Mr. Aberlour was given an anesthetic and had vague impressions of drowning before he conked out. The surgery was brief and successful. Dr. Persaud worked nimbly with his various instruments, and within minutes Mr. Aberlour’s foreskin lay at the bottom of a little plastic jar like a piece of discarded chicken fat.

That evening Mrs. Aberlour drove the car home from the hospital. Mr. Aberlour sat in the front seat looking uncomfortable. He kept shifting as if to cross his legs, wince, and then straighten them again.

(cut)

Gavin Mitchell:

> *“Here we encounter the inevitable man-with-rock, standing erect in his old Freudian realm.”*
>
> \- Cixous

Eighteen year-old Gavin Mitchell, whose circumcised penis measured three and one-quarter inches flaccid, and doubled to six and one-half inches erect, had recently moved out of his parents' house and into a Glenelg flat with his girlfriend, Sandra. They would both be starting at Adelaide Uni together in the fall. Sandra was an avid rollerblader. Gavin’s skin was the exact colour of a “Flesh” pencil crayon, and he had an impressive collection of empty liquor bottles lined up like trophies on the living room mantel.

Sandra and Gavin had been dating for eight months. They had fornicated for the first time to mark the six-month point in their relationship. While it had been Gavin's first sexual experience,

Sandra had lost her virginity three years prior to a German exchange student named Klaus. They had done it in a field and Klaus had reassured her by saying, "Don't worry, the penetration will be pleasurable," and then he had spread his red denim jacket down on the grass underneath them.

Sandra had found her first bout of intercourse with Gavin somewhat unsatisfying, and candidly let him know he would have to improve. Gavin was hurt, but resolved to do better. He loved Sandra. The first time they had done it he had been surprised by some of the noises produced, but had proceeded unperturbed, lest he should be revealed as somehow inadequate. Since then it had become his mission to gratify his girlfriend, not only to ensure her happiness, but also to bolster his own self-esteem. Admittedly, he was improving.

Recently, after a particularly successful bout of love-making, Sandra had flopped onto her side of the bed with a gasp and exclaimed: "Wow! I guess size really doesn't matter!" At the time Gavin had been absorbed with mopping up a puddle of semen with his t-shirt, and had laughed the remark off. The following day, however, he began to think about what Sandra had said, and he became confused.

Gavin was unsure whether Sandra's comment was meant as a compliment. Regardless, she was insinuating that he had a small penis. Sandra more often saw Gavin's penis in its flaccid, three and one-quarter inch state; when it was fully erect, and doubled in length, the penis was usually inside Sandra's vagina, where it became impossible to get a good look at. Its growth, however, even Gavin himself found nothing short of remarkable. He wondered if Sandra was aware of just how impressive the increase in size actually was.

In the following few days Gavin found himself plagued by dreams of his penis falling off. In these dreams he was usually able to retrieve it, but the re-attachment presented itself as somewhat of an ordeal.

In one dream, he discovered his penis in one of the opal jewelers on Hindley Street. He went into the store, and there it was, resting on a velvet cushion inside a glass cabinet. In another, he opened up his refrigerator to discover his penis standing upright behind a jug of milk. It was odd, and rather disconcerting.

Gavin became sullen and stalked around the apartment. He watched a great deal of television, refused to wash his dishes, and avoided going outside. This was unfortunate, as the weather at the time was quite lovely. Sandra spent most of her days zipping around town on her rollerblades. This Gavin resented. He knew the type of men she would be meeting on Adelaide's boardwalks — those muscular, tanned in-line skater-types, flaunting their ample members in lycra cycling shorts. In the evenings Sandra would return home sweaty and grinning, having obviously enjoyed another afternoon of admiring gigantic penises. Gavin found the entire business sickening.

Gavin awoke one day to his alarm, set for 11:30 a.m., and Sandra was standing over him. She wore her rollerblades, which made her look about seven feet tall.

"What's up with you?"

"What do you mean?" said Gavin. He rubbed some sleep from his eyes and sat up in bed.

"You know what I'm talking about."

Gavin said nothing.

"I'm going rollerblading," Sandra announced, and glided out of the room.

Gavin was left alone. The front door slammed as Sandra wheeled out into the midday sun.

Gavin got out of bed. He showered, vaguely recalling a dream from the night before in which his penis had been stolen by a gang of kilted Scotsmen. Gavin had tracked them down to a local pub, but the details from that point on were foggy.

Gavin dressed, tucking his penis carefully into his trousers. He checked his wallet for cash, and was pleased to discover $80.

(cut)

Alice Nguyen

> *"Unlike man, who holds so dearly to his title and his titles, his pouches of value, his cap, crown, and everything connected with his head, woman couldn't care less about the fear of decapitation (or castration), adventuring, without the masculine temerity, into anonymity, which she can merge with, without annihilating herself."*
>
> - Cixous

Alice Nguyen was nine, lived right by Brighton Beach, and didn't really know what a penis was. Consensus among her friends seemed to be that it was the bit of meat that hung between the boys' legs, and this is what they peed out of, but the logistics of the penis eluded her. One Saturday morning Alice woke up determined to find out.

Alice's father had disappeared when she was a baby in Vietnam. Alice had promptly been whisked off to Australia by her mother, Quynh, who now lived and worked in Adelaide as a photographer on one of the city's weeklies. Quynh spoke impeccable English (better, she felt, than most Australians) and felt oddly elated whenever a Beach Boys' song came on the radio, especially "Help Me Rhonda." Male influence in Alice's life was minimal. It was just her and her mother, and neither of them had penises.

There were of course the penises on the boys at school, but those were usually covered up by some form of clothing. Alice was at least certain that the penises would be unleashed to urinate. Out of curiosity she had once wandered into the boys' toilets at school and witnessed the bizarre contraptions on the walls that looked like misshapen sinks. Apparently the boys pointed their penises into the sinks and peed. Alice found this equally hilarious and repugnant.

Still, Alice was intent on seeing a penis. And as she lay in bed on this particular Saturday morning, the sun slicing in through the venetian blinds of her bedroom window, Alice quickly devised a plan. To begin, Alice got up and went directly into the kitchen, where her mother sat with a cup of coffee, the newspaper spread out in front of her. It was 8:40.

"I need a haircut," Alice announced.

Quynh continued reading. "You just had a haircut."

"I want it short."

Her mother looked up. "How short?"

"Here." Alice gestured with her hand to an area somewhere above her ear.

"That is short," said Alice's mother, and then went back to the paper.

"I want it short. It's summer soon."

"Can I do it after lunch?"

"No," said Alice. "Now."

At precisely 9:08 Alice stood in front of the bathroom mirror, trying to decide if she had made a mistake. Her hair was indeed very short. Boy short. Alice smiled. Hair grows back, she thought to herself, and then remarked how mature a sentiment it was for a girl her age.

Then Alice went into the living room and telephoned her friend Roxan, whose parents had named their daughter after a popular song, but had misspelled the name on the birth certificate. Roxan was eight and preferred to be called "Rox." She carried a purse, always.

"Rox," said Alice.

"Hiya." Roxan sounded half asleep.

"Let's go swimming."

"What time is it?"

"At the pool, not at the beach. Can your dad take us?"

"Swimming?"

"Ask." Alice was getting impatient.

"Hold on," said Roxan, and there was a fumbling sort of noise from the other end, and then Roxan's muffled voice yelling something. She returned.

"Yeah, we can go. But after lunch. We'll pick you up."

"Good," said Alice, and hung up the phone. Everything,

finally, was falling into place.

Alice spent the rest of the morning preparing herself. She assembled on the kitchen table a number of what, from hearsay, she gathered to be phallic-shaped objects — a carrot, a pencil, two chopsticks, a handful of toothpicks. She stared at them, trying to imagine them attached to the crotches of human beings. It seemed absurd. Alice went to the refrigerator and poured herself a glass of milk.

Alice's mother came into the kitchen, noticed her daughter's collection and smiled. "I can make you some lunch, if you're hungry."

"It's too late," said Alice. "You're meant to eat at least one hour before you swim."

"Right," said her mother, who then went out into the backyard to water the plants.

(cut)

SHAUNA MCKENNA

Shauna McKenna's work has been printed in *Pindeldyboz* and *Monkeybicycle*, and featured online at the *Mississippi Review*, *Eyeshot*, *Reinventing the World*, among others. She's never been serenaded.

likes	dislikes
Blather, Superspy Sydney Bristow, Snarky evasions	Tomato slime, Physical exertion, The dogs of capitalism

Chance

Hated the whole thing, having to go to the private lessons, having to haul the heavy wood and polyester velvet-lined case around, knocking against legs, sheet music jammed in backpack with crumpled brownbag lunch and creased homework, having to go, hating it like all the other kids, tired of the same singsong refrains from her mother, "someday you'll thank me for this," never believing, hating to hear it, hating to go, hating to wait while the student before her finished, for many years a chubby boy named Alfie, then a shy kid, a girl with olive skin and chestnut braids whose name she doesn't remember, then no one, because apparently Mr. McDaniel had a break between lessons, and she'd come upon him with a dishcloth in hand, or the radio still fanning wide across his single-level house, or a pressed look to his face, as if he'd been sleeping, or maybe lying flat.

But then, after years had passed, and Mr. McDaniel seemed starchier, more crinkled, she began to love it. She spent long hours closed in her bedroom, away from her sister, her mother, her father, all captive to the burble of the TV; she worked through a series of notes until they bent her fingers automatically, like a pulse; she practiced, she played; she practiced, she played.

It was the same with Michael. Had thought, too skinny. Too angled. No grace, no ease. Always aware, always sensitive to every breath in the room, every change in tone, every frown, every insinuation. Not the least bit smooth. Doesn't remember when they met. Of course she doesn't remember when they met, it's not the kind of thing, when you've known each other from elementary school onward, when he's always been there, it's not anything she would ever remember, the exact day they met.

They worked together on a project in English class. She didn't mind. It didn't bother her. She didn't specifically dislike him; she just wasn't interested, or so she thought, or rather so she didn't think, before that project. It was a speech. They did a speech on mitosis. The topic was assigned to them by the teacher. Patricia had no interest in cellular division. Michael was okay with the topic; in fact he was downright enthusiastic. He came to her house the day after the project was assigned, walked home with her. He spoke while they were walking about genetics, specifically genomes, on which he'd done an individual science project in fall semester that Mr. Angelo had awarded with an "A"; he knew, he said, he knew that Patty ("Patricia," she said, or "Tricia,") he knew that Patricia knew there was a difference between genes and genomes. Patricia shrugged, he stayed silent the rest of the way; could be he thought she was ignorant, could be he worried about having possibly insulted her.

The speech went well, the project went well, they got along great. So great, in fact, that they started eating lunch together in the school cafeteria. Patricia discovered herself pleased that they had the same lunch period, the school was divided into three, staggered groups, and even though right at first she wouldn't let on how much she looked forward to seeing him, she found herself counting down and finally she had to say, well that's what's what, and invited him to meet her at a baseball game after school. His eyes bulged, he said yes, it hadn't occurred to him to go, but go he did. She sat alone on the bleachers, away from her sister, away from her friend Allison, both of whom were given strict instructions not to stare, the side of her hand against her forehead veiling the low-slung sun, peering toward the school exit to see who came next. When she spotted him, she jumped to her feet, waving, beckoning for him to make his way to her side. He was so pleased. She was so pleased.

***

Sun livid in the trees. Breath in the lungs like woodsmoke. Stink of her body, stink of fright. Crackle, the brother. Crackle, the father.

Shape hanging between the two. A spine in man's clothing. A leg with a foot. A shape.

***

Very fortunate that she started loving the violin, now, because you have to love something, you have to be into something, you have to have some shorthand of yourself, like swimmer or cheerleader, or goth, or punk, or partier, or speech maker, or Ivy League contender, or worker at Banana Republic, or weekend waitress, or poetry writer, or wild child scooting down to the City at every opportunity to hang out in the park, laugh at the tourists, screw between the trees… you have to be something. So that's what she was. A violinist. And according to Mr. McDaniel, a very good one, not that he said it often, so clutching with compliments, doling them out between intervals of weeks, months even, saying it softly while stroking his rust-spotted hands, avoiding eye contact. She didn't doubt her worth, had a blast at private recitals and school symphony performances, even competed in the state contest, came second.

Patricia helped cook on Saturday evenings. Listened to Prairie Home Companion with her mother. Earlier in the day, the two of them poring over a cookbook, Patricia scanning the cupboards to confirm or deny the presence of needed ingredients and her mother scratching out a grocery list with a pencil and notepad she kept on top of the refrigerator. Then the trip to the grocery store, crowded on a Saturday, no time to chat, debating which direction to turn the cart, almost a race, a test to see if they could get through the aisles and grab everything on the list in one winding sweep, without having to double back, pick up whatever was missed from the first time around. In the car on the way out they would listen to classical music; sometimes Patricia's mother would talk about the way it was in Texas, where she grew up. They watched people on the sidewalks, in the other cars.

Music, their shared dialect. The music in the car, operatic violins and twiddling flutes, the music while cooking. Prairie Home Companion, bluegrass, soloists, folk. One week a band with a strange name. The Klezmatics. Patricia thought it was funny, sounded like phlegm, thought they were trying for funny. But they weren't, they were earnest, playing traditional Jewish music, like she'd seen on Fiddler on the Roof, except bright, boisterous, strong, immediate. She paused in what she was doing, grating a carrot, asked her mother if she knew much about this kind of music. Her mother said no, but that she thought it was nice, and poured oil into a wok that sizzled like a laugh. It was okay, the show was in the middle of an instrumental by Guy's All-Star Shoe Band, but as soon as the carrots were done Patricia asked her mother if she didn't mind she'd leave and her mother shrugged, flexible as always, while Patricia raced up the stairs to her room to catch the rest of the show uninterrupted.

***

Started reading about it, got CD's of the Klezmatics, Brave Old World, on a Long Island Railroad journey to the City one weekend, found a specialty music store, nice selection, willing to order more, got the old stuff, reconstructions of the old stuff, what they would have been listening to in Europe, the Jews of the diaspora, scattered somewhat but concentrated in pockets of Russia, Poland, hiding but living, klezmers moving from town to town, playing, while straining under religious and secular restrictions, the musical expressions of common happiness and common prayer and common love. Learned about the original klezmer as migrated to the United States, performing by memory, a funhouse mirror of the Old World life, replete with recognizable elements but different, crowded in tenements, no path to the woods, shtetl but not-shtetl; then the Klezmer Revivalist, after the music of refuge had been hushed, ignored, passed over in the attempt to assimilate, by the generation of this world, of America, willfully forgetting then anxiously recovering, the generation of searchers, of young men and women working at identity like a jigsaw puzzle of pride; then finally, the years when Patricia stumbled into it, stumbled happily there, the years of Renaissance, of claiming, of saying this is mine, and I share it with you, of this is ours, of this is unfettered, of this is old and something I'm making from the point of origin, fresh, as I live forward, as I waltz with time, as I continue, as I learn, as I compose, as I play. Voices that sung laughter, that sung loss, instruments that spoke words, rhythms like the muscular heart, beating.

***

What was happening was that Michael was enthralled, thinking about her, but satisfied enough with the what was happening and the way it was happening that he didn't feel the need to hound her, to get her to accede more more more, to get her to want more more more, it was fine, just fine, they hung out on the weekends, sometimes studied or listened to music together during the week, it was all okay. She had a long, graceful body. He felt ashamed that when he called her to mind, that was the first thing his mind rested on, the first in a series of rubrics, the long line of her body from curving calf to oval head, draped like a veil by hazelnut hair. Then he would think of her smile, a good smile, maybe a bit wider than fashionable, the teeth somewhat prominent, but what the smile meant was what they were sharing, the laughter. She was surprisingly sarcastic, surprising he figured because she was so soft to people on first impression, but her sense of irony biting, relentless. Nothing sacred to her. He accompanied her to her grandmother's funeral. She wasn't really mourning, wasn't really close to her grandmother, who'd lived in a nursing home for the last fifteen years and had been estranged from Patricia's father, the visits obligatory, but rare. At the funeral Michael and Patricia sat in the back, he, awfully uncomfortable. Natural for anybody to be uncomfortable, but he'd never been in a church before, couldn't keep up with all the standing, then sitting, then kneeling, then the singing of the hymns, and Patricia didn't help much, holding the hymnal open in front of them, chirping along in her on-key, but weak, singing voice, giving him no hint of reprieve. He recognized the chorus and tried to contribute a few notes. When the hymn finished, people shuffling out of pews, Patricia patted his knee and whispered, "You're one of us now; come eat some Jesus," and she let him blanch and stare at her too long before giggling and pecking him on the cheek to let him know she was kidding.

***

Sharp voice, the German. His buddies, soldier friends, laughing. Slaps on the back. Rifle rising like a machine, unstoppable force. Crack. She screamed.

***

Just had to get through it. Practice not always a joy. So long she had hated it, then liked it in the main, but with the advancing tiers of difficulty came real frustration, frustration that sent her meeting her worst self; her most faithless self. Mr. McDaniel, no help. He almost seemed mirthful, attending to his tea while she complained about the difficulties. "Someday you'll realize that struggle is the best part of experience. It's friction, dear. Without it, you wouldn't be able to measure joy." Not making any sense. She was saying, what she was trying to say, was that sometimes it was so hard, sometimes she didn't think she was up to the task, she knew exactly how it had to sound in the end, she had volumes of classical recordings to listen to, had the memories of nights at Lincoln Center with music that would roll over her like a perfumed dusk, rattle her like the firing of rifles. She knew how she was supposed to be, how she was supposed to make it be, and she also knew that she was close, but not there yet. "For heaven's sake, Patricia. You're working on Bach. You have to keep at it. Nobody gets Bach without a lot of practice." But no relief, because at night she'd have to face the music stand, have to hold her violin, and panic. Panic. After dinner the night following her lesson she picked it up, put it down, and called Michael instead. Disgusted when she went to bed, had a hard time sleeping.

***

"I can't relate," he said, when she played him some klezmer. "What do you mean, you can't relate? To the music?" she asked, mystified and irritated, because she knew what he meant, he wasn't saying exactly what he meant, it wasn't that he couldn't relate, it was that he related in a different way than he wanted to explain to her, which was fine, if only he said it that way, admitted the truth. Because he was Jewish, and she wasn't. And he wouldn't offend her by saying that she couldn't understand, but offended her anyway with the half-truth.

When he left, she hopped online to research exchange programs to Poland. She clicked through link after link, first about the programs themselves, then about Polish history, and then specifically about Holocaust history. Only random chance that she was who she was. She bowed her head and slept through time's winding back. She slept and her eyes opened onto something that shrieked to life, ashes from ashes, bones walking new now, locked into joints, one step, the next step.

***

Under her fingernails, dirt and blood. Saw them disappearing behind the corner, then the man stepping out, coming her way, pleading with her, "Little girl, little girl, keep quiet, we won't harm you, we won't steal anything, keep quiet, keep quiet," Ran out of the barn and the brown-suited soldiers came as a pair, jogging, one grinned at her, winked, raised his fingers to his lips to signal her to hush, she froze, switched directions, ran some more. Dirt in grains, blood from the small cuts of gravel. She ran behind a stand of trees, dove to the ground, watched. Seconds after the soldiers entered the barn, two small boys, flying, flying, toward the meadow. The whipcrack sound of a rifle shot. One soldier emerged, raised his rifle to his shoulder, took aim. Another whipcrack. The taller of the two boys fell as if slapped down. The shorter boy kept going, whipcrack, whipcrack, again, again. He made the field. The other soldier came out of the barn. The shooter lowered his rifle. Together they went over to the clump of dark clothes and black hair fluttering. One soldier nudged the body with his foot. She couldn't tell if it was the same soldier who told her to shush. The soldiers left the body, left the barnyard, chattering in German. She stayed until dark. She saw her mother come from the house and stand over the body a long time, cross herself. Then her father and her brother went into the barn, reappeared with the slack figure of the man stretched between them, came toward her in the woods. Passed nearby, leaves and branches rustling under their heavy tread, their solemn march. She followed the sound of them until it faded off; then silence for a while, then the rustling of their return. Took the body of the child. A plot in the woods. She stayed until dark. Her mother calling to her during the forest burial, after, every few minutes until the girl decided to return. Couldn't say anything, and was surprised how little her mother scolded her. Embraced her, even. A dark sleep, woken to a dawn of horrible regret. Never went back to the woods. Never.

***

Michael came over a few days later without calling. She got the door, he stood on the porch, the beautiful autumn day swarming with leaves behind him. The muscles in his face were tight. She couldn't tell if he was angry or distressed. By now she thought she would have known. Six months. Maureen had graduated, was living in the city with her boyfriend. Patricia greeted him and stepped back into the house, assuming he would follow. He didn't, stood there on the step, rigid.

"Michael, what?" she asked, though she knew. It wasn't small, the fight they had. It wasn't a long exchange, and nothing nasty was said, but they never fought, so as far as they were concerned any disruption of their peace was catastrophic, requiring immediate repair before life could continue as normal. She knew this, but pretended not to know. She didn't want it to be the case. She was tired. Wanted to practice. Right now, wanted only to feel her violin tucked between shoulder and chin. Wanted to get good. Wanted to get perfect.

"Tricia, this might be the only chance we have. For the rest of our lives. If you go to Europe next year, we might lose it."

She rubbed her thumb against the doorframe, avoiding his eye. Of course she knew he was right. At that moment she didn't care, was tired.

"I don't want to decide everything for the rest of my life right now, Michael. That's just not fair. Now are you coming in?"

Michael lingered. A breeze cut through his hair, he relaxed, pulled Patricia to him, kissed her cheek. He went in, and that was that, for the time.

***

Good morning. Seize the day. Do what you have to do. Be true to yourself. May the road rise to you. Wherever you go, there you are. Today is the first day of the rest of your life. All we need is love. Give peace a chance. Make love, not war. Get your laws off my body.

Straight but not narrow. Just say no. Mean people suck. Video killed the radio star. The revolution will not be televised. Kill your television. It's the end of the world as we know it. Do they know it's Christmas time at all? Kiss them for me. No means no. If you're attacked yell fire. No one knows what it's like to be the bad man, to be the sad man, behind blue eyes. Till he cried out in his anger and his pain, I am bleeding, I am bleeding, but the fighter still remains, still remains. Six million. I'll be back. Fuck me gently with a chainsaw. Welcome to the jungle. Just like heaven. Oh, the places you'll go. Our father who art in heaven. I think, therefore. So much depends on. Wherefore art thou. I am slain. Hosanna, heysanna. Another suitcase, and another hall. Jane says. Summertime rolls.

***

At what point in the process it became irreversible she doesn't remember. Came home from school one day, saw the envelope from the Polish Embassy with her visa papers inside, realized that all the trouble she'd gone to had made it permanent, made it real, made it inevitable. Going to Poland the next year.

***

Never came home. Left the woods. Then left the home.

***

Like a vacuum. No time. Nothing moved. She sat on gray polyester-blend chairs, bolted in a row, looking out the terminal windows as huge steel birds rolled forward, lights blinking. Riding to the airport, she had sat in the middle seat, Michael and Maureen flanking her. The whole time her mother and father and Maureen chattered about what they'd heard of Polish life, wondered what she'd do with her foster brother and much younger foster sister, what kind of meals would be cooked for dinner. Patricia's mother joked that she and her father would starve on Saturdays. You could hear how hard she was trying to be cheerful. Hard to look at Michael, see his bumpy profile that she knew so soon she would be missing. Looked at him once, he squeezed her hand harder. Almost cried.

But in the terminal, without time, without change, it all seemed perfect. Family and Michael vanished to a different region, even though they were at that moment only miles away on the expressway heading home. Pulled the map of Warsaw from her bag, looked at the names, address and strange phone number of her new foster family. She'd spoken with the mother, Kat, in a jumble of broken Polish exchanged with broken English. It was a conversation from the other side of today, and she'd played her violin for half an hour in joy as a way of saying her excitement.

The violin was staying home. Made her cringe to think of it, like Michael. Shrugged it off, with effort.

A stocky woman wearing an American Airlines uniform fiddled with the microphone at the terminal gate. Patricia pulled her ticket from her purse. She took note of her seat number so she could queue at the right time: 13F. She watched the woman rustle papers on a clipboard. Patricia's breath hovered in the top of her lungs, right at the intersection with her throat.

Lump of clothes, bundle of limbs. Airplane pushing through clouds. Scratches under nails, acid fright drying in muscles. Violin inert. Father and brother carrying, to the woods. Air gone cold, finally she rises. Left and never returned.

Elizabeth Ellen

Elizabeth Ellen is currently obsessed with finding a pair of sunglasses like the ones worn by Uma Thurman in *Kill Bill Vol. 2* (you know, the ones she wears while talking to Michael Parks in that kickass scene which David Denby deemed "unnecessary."). Unfortunately, she has no idea what brand of sunglasses these might be, nor where she might purchase them even if she did know. She knows only that they make Uma look really, really hot, even hotter than she normally does, which is still really hot. Anyone with this information is encouraged to forward it to elizabethellen@mac.com. Elizabeth realizes that she could probably find this information out for herself with a bit of googling, but she is lazy and you live for this sort of shit. She knows this about you. And she thanks you in advance.

likes

remembering, barefoot, strippers (female), Jay-Z, sea anemones, Key West, stories by JT LeRoy, Ann Cummins and Stephany Aulenback, Ms. Pacman, Irish whiskey, dorks, sneaking Charleston Chews into movies, forgetting

dislikes

forgetting, shoes, strippers (male), phony rappers, sea monkeys, the rest of Florida, stories left on your answering machine by your less-than-sober grandmother (requiring numerous messages in which to tell them, causing you to believe momentarily (when you come home and find the number six blinking on your machine) that you are more popular than you had thought, until the playing of said messages reminds you that you are just as unpopular as ever and that Grandma drinks too much on Sunday afternoons), getting your ass kicked at Ms. Pacman by a seven year old, Bailey's, cool kids, when your date sneaks only one Charleston Chew into the movie and suddenly you are really hungry, remembering.

The Girl at the End of the Bar

The backseat of the '57 Volvo sedan was still cold, the aged heater unable to provide enough warmth to prevent the girl from seeing her own breath. It was the winter of the great blizzard, though only hints of its imminent arrival were yet visible through the frosted windows. On the other side of the glass the snow was falling in a leisurely manner, pacing itself for the accelerated speed to come. In the closed mouth of the girl seated in back, the tongue was drawn to the new void, filling the space left from the tooth that had been spat out earlier in the day between mouthfuls of Cream of Wheat. As the car bumped along the dirt road under a canopy of trees planted long ago in the days of Johnny Appleseed, the girl's mind was on the tooth, fallen and lone, there in a tissue on the table beside her bed, waiting for her to return and place it under her pillow.

Upfront, the grown ups sat, the mother and the Wolfman, silent in their own thoughts that did not involve lost teeth or the taste of blood. The Wolfman had entered their lives two years prior, on the eve of the country's bicentennial. He came dressed in denim, beneath a beard that was allowed to grow at will, the same as the hair that flowed over his suede collar. He brought with him, into their living room, the Loyalists, the men they knew only as Smoke and Squirrel, Goofy and Sweet, Hog and Red. These were the men who took the girl upon their knees, who brought her forbidden sweets and told the girl that their hearts were reserved for her. These were the men who told her jokes and made her giggle until the hour was late, the smoke in the wood-heated living room thick, and the mother made her climb the stairs, feet dragging, to bed.

Before the Wolfman there had been two other men. One, the father, had come and gone, staying only long enough for the girl's conception, leaving a single photograph and a mere hint of a memory. The second man, the only one the girl ever called Daddy, had remained longer, long enough to see her walk and talk, to teach her to ride a bike and wave goodbye. In fact, it had been the mother who had left him, in a newly constructed house meant to be their home, in a state they had moved to together, for a fresh start. She had packed their bags and taken the girl with her, though the girl hadn't wished to go, had wanted only to stay and play Go Fish, to eat cold hot dogs and watch basketball with her Daddy, though he wasn't, the mother now reminded her, really her dad. But the mother's will was strong and the girl but a girl. She had taken hold the mother's hand and not looked back.

In the backseat of the car that kept chugging along, the girl might have been thinking of the left behind man, of showing him her tooth with its bit of dried blood at the root. Then again, she might not have been thinking of him at all. The mother had turned on the F.M. and the girl was concentrating on the fifty ways to leave a lover. She wondered how many of these ways the mother had already used, of how many more she might use in the future. She wondered if the Wolfman were wondering the same thing.

The parking lot was already full when they pulled into a space between familiar trucks and cars. The sky was darkening and the snow was falling with increased velocity and greater weight than before. The girl opened her mouth and stuck out her tongue, tasting the coolness as they made their way to the door. She had to run to catch up. The mother and the Wolfman were already half inside, waiting for her to enter into the smoky warmth of the bar.

Inside, the Loyalists were gathered, seated aside one another on the usual stools. It was a Friday night and so their pockets were full, their bellies well on their way to being immersed in brew. Some weekend nights the girl stayed at her grandparents' playing Tiddly

Winks and eating ice cream. Other times, as was the case this evening, she chose to remain with the mother, which more often than not, meant accompanying her and the Wolfman here, where quarters were handed out freely, a jukebox and pinball machines awaiting their deposit.

A couple of the Loyalists traded seats, opening up three barstools in a row, one for each of them. The mother chose the one in the middle and the girl and the Wolfman sat down on either side of her. A rootbeer was placed in front of the girl and she reached across Sweet for the jar of pretzel rods, taking only two for starters. Sitting quietly she listened half-heartedly to the grown ups talk of jobs lost and garnered, of women yearned for and bemoaned, all the while dipping the pretzels deep into her soda before sucking off the salt and eating the mushy remains. When the first two had been hastily consumed two more were procured, then another two, until finally the mother, remembering the girl to her right, asked if she were hungry. A pizza burger and fries were ordered for the girl, though the adults seemed sated by their steady stream of drinks and cigarettes.

By the time the food arrived the mother and the Wolfman were back on their feet, playing pool first for fun and then for money. The girl took pride in noting that the mother's game was superior not only to the Wolfman's, but to just about everyone else's in the joint. Sitting with her back to the bar, the burger on her lap, the girl watched the mother. She studied her stance, observed her steady stroke, silently applauded her coolness under pressure. The mother, as anyone could plainly see, was a thing of beauty. The straight, brown hair, normally allowed to fall freely upon her shoulders, was pulled back off her face. The catlike, green eyes, speckled with bits of amber, were focused downward, to the end of the stick, unwavering. The body that was at once athletic and curved was bent but straight, frozen in perfect form, drawing all eyes from nearby tables and stools. One day, the girl thought. I hope to be half the woman she is. Then I will be happy.

It had been seven and a half years that the girl had known the mother. Seven and a half years since she'd been pushed out from the comfort of her womb, since she'd gasped those first breaths independent of the mother. Ever since she'd wanted only to return to the drowned safety within. At every opportunity she'd taken hold the mother's hand, climbed into her lap, crawled into her bed, needing the physical proximity, craving the warmth of the mother's skin against her own tepid body. For seven and a half years the girl had thought only of ways to earn the mother's love. Every crude finger-painting, every ceramic ashtray, every dandelion bouquet — all had been for the mother — attempts at extracting more love.

And in the interims, between men, it seemed the girl was almost sated, nearly quieted. She and the mother would become inseparable; her hand was tightly grasped, nightly visits to the mother's bed were allowed, and she happily, or greedily, became the mother's sole source of love. But the mother was not merely a mother. The mother, too, was a woman, bound by the laws and desires of her womanhood. The girl recognized these desires in the mother and loathed them. She loathed them because she was helpless to fulfill them. She loathed herself because she was not a man. She loathed the men because they could give the mother what she never could, not with all her stupid drawings and misshapen vases and whispered "I love you's." The girl loathed the men and herself because she could never loathe the mother. Sharing the mother, it seemed, was a prerequisite for loving her.

And now the most recent of these men, the Wolfman, appeared before the girl, bearing a grin and an open hand stacked neatly with quarters. In his beard, the girl noticed, was a bit of foam from the beer he held in his other. His eyes twinkled as the department store Santa's should have but didn't and the girl found it impossible to remain on the other side of those eyes, that grin, without smiling back herself, though she didn't want to. Smiling was admitting acceptance. Acceptance led to love. Love led to abandonment and, ultimately, heartache. She took the quarters and stifled a grin. The Wolfman touched her cheek, then lit a Kool and returned to the Loyalists further down the bar.

Setting aside the unwanted remains of her sandwich, she slid down the front of the stool, quarters tucked neatly into her sweaty palm, and made her way over to the jukebox. There were few more satisfying sounds than the tinkle of quarters hitting the metal innards of a jukebox. She chose carefully the five songs that her money afforded her. She hoped silently that one of her choices might please the mother, might cause her to hum or sing along as she sipped her scotch from across the room, as she draped her lithe body over the pool table. But it was not the mother's singing voice that met the girl's ears as she stood with her back turned, two selections remaining, her first, "Fly Like An Eagle," already filling the bar. Instead it was the sound of the scotch in her throat, the voice that in the confines of their home encouraged the girl to shut off the television and quietly make her way up the stairs to her bedroom, shutting the door tight behind her. Here in the bar, she dared not turn around. She concentrated all her efforts on finding two more songs to fill the room, two more songs to drown out the alcohol laden threats being heralded from across the hazy room, not at her, but invoking fear in her all the same. As she pushed in the last numbers she felt a hand on her shoulder. Turning hesitantly around, she found it was not the mother, as she had both hoped and feared, but Skinny, another Loyalist, the one that seemed to like her best of them all.

He was smiling down at her from his 6'3" stance. He was asking her if she wanted to join him in a game of pinball. He was saving her. She nodded appreciatively and trailed behind as he made his way through the sea of escalated voices and extinguished cigarette butts. The corner of the room in which the pinball was located was quieter and darker than the rest of the place, a bit isolated and removed.

She stood on the stool beside the machine, watching Skinny's long frame hunched over, hugging the flippers, gently maneuvering the ball where he wanted it to go. She thought of all the times he had come to their house, bringing her chocolate-covered graham crackers, knowing they were her favorite, knowing the mother would never allow her to place a box of them in their grocery cart on shopping day. She thought of how he'd sit her on his lap while he talked to the Wolfman about the proceeding night's poker game or an upcoming canoe trip. She thought about how he didn't have a little girl of his own, nor a wife, not even a woman. It seemed unfair, that such a nice guy should be so alone. She wondered if, perhaps, he might be the next man to infiltrate their lives, if and when the mother tired of the Wolfman. Were it up to her, he would be. He wouldn't have to pretend to like her. He wouldn't have to buy her a puppy to make her like him.

He played her three games then placed in her hand the quarters that remained before apologizing and explaining that he had to go and work the night shift, that he was damn near late already. She watched him go, watched as he said goodbye to the Wolfman first, and then the mother, who were standing on opposite sides of the bar. Their separation seemed not to be accidental. The girl played one more game then pocketed the rest of the quarters for later.

The bar was at capacity now. She made her way through the familiar and unfamiliar faces, smiling shyly when someone she knew or was supposed to know acknowledged her with a nod or a waved "hello." She continued pushing past, until she found the table she liked best, the one wooden picnic table into which someone had carved a semicircle, creating a seat for those with child. She slid onto the bench, felt the soft curve of the wood, wondering momentarily what it might be like to embody a belly large enough to fill the void, a belly in which another life was growing by the day, by the hour. Pulling her out of this image was her eye, now drawn to the mural which hung before her, just overhead, a mural she had stared at so many nights in the past, immersed in its rendering of a war fought between whites and Indians. She studied once more the blood and wounds, the scalps and felled men. She was transfixed by the violence depicted, intrigued by the actual act of scalping, of the entire hairline being sliced off like the unwanted top of a late-summer tomato. There were hundreds of men and horses and bodies strewn interwoven and tangled throughout the painting. As she tried in vain to count the fallen bodies as she had many times in the past, the mother's voice echoed from behind, carried over the other patrons, finding her, reaching her distant ears, reminding her of why it was she was feigning invisibility.

The words, however, as always, were unavoidable, and as the girl listened reluctantly she realized that a disagreement of sorts had broken out between the Wolfman, the mother, and a third person, a man unrecognizable to the girl. The last time she had heard the mother's voice reach this octave, she had discovered the next morning that their television had been kicked in, rendered unusable. The mother was a woman of uncontainable passion and questionable judgment, both of which seemed only to be exacerbated by the intake of scotch. Having no bedroom into which to retreat, the girl walked quietly, eyes averted, toward the bathroom.

It was, as you would expect a bar bathroom to be, dimly lit and devoid of anything but the most basic of facilities. There were two stalls. The first toilet had been left unflushed, and so the girl took the second. She closed the faded green metal door behind her and sat down on the open toilet with her overalls still fastened. She didn't have to pee, she realized. Instead she read the words that had been carved onto the door, words a seven year old probably shouldn't know, yet were not foreign to her vocabulary. With an outstretched finger she felt the scratched grooves that the writer of the letters had managed to form, rather elementarily, a bit off kilter. The metal was cold. She pressed her flushed cheek to it. She stood that way, cheek to door, alternating sides periodically when her body heat had warmed that particular square of metal, until the sound of the bathroom door swinging open interrupted her thoughts, which were of nothing in particular, which were meditative in nature. Footsteps bogged down in boots with two-inch heels fought their own weight in an effort to reach the stall closest the door in as few steps as possible. The woman to whom the boots belonged did not seem to mind or notice the unflushed toilet. The girl, looking now at the floor, looking curiously under the wall that separated the stalls, noted that the woman's feet were turned in the wrong direction, or at least, in the opposite direction from which a person usually places them when seated on a toilet. Soon she knew why. She covered her ears and turned her face to the opposite corner of the stall as the sound and stench of the liquid contents of the woman's stomach hitting the water filled the room.

After the toilet had been flushed more than once and the woman's feet had been turned in the appropriate direction, the girl looked down once more. She recognized the boots. She had been with the Wolfman when he bought them a few weeks back, just before Christmas. The boots left the stall and made their way to the sink, seemingly unaware of any other presence in the bathroom. The girl listened to the sound of running water being splashed and drank. A purse was unzipped and the sound of something being inhaled filled the cement block walls. The girl thought of the snuff the mother and the Wolfman sometimes snorted when the men filled their living room on cold, winter nights such as this. And then, as quickly as she had appeared, the woman was gone, the door swung shut behind her, the girl left to herself once more.

It was getting late and the girl was growing tired. She wondered how much longer they would be staying. She didn't want to miss the Tooth Fairy. She went ahead and emptied her bladder, since she was already there. She left the stall and went to the sink. She washed her hands and looked somewhat absently at the girl peering back at her. She thought of how grown ups were always telling her she'd break a lot of hearts someday, "with those big, blue eyes of yours." But she knew they were wrong. Her body and face were already changing, already betraying her. She barely recognized herself. She missed the cute, little girl she had once been — the one the mother had taken pleasure in dressing. No longer was she fussed over, no more was her hair braided or put into hot rollers or pigtails. Now her hair hung limp and neglected. The girl pushed it out of her eyes and walked out of the bathroom. She still had a few quarters in her pocket.

What she heard upon exiting, however, nearly had her turning right back around and heading once more for the safety of her stall. But she didn't. She was sick of hiding. In the midst of the chaos she returned to the jukebox, returned to the comfort of familiar music.

As she deposited the quarters pulled from her pocket, she heard the mother and the Wolfman exchanging words, some of which she recognized from the metal door she had only just read. Mostly it was the mother talking, screaming. The Wolfman appeared, as usual, to be losing the battle. The girl almost felt sorry for him. She knew what it was to be the object of the scotch-infused rage. For the moment she was thankful not to be the one on the opposite side of those maddened eyes.

The Wolfman strolled over to the juxe box, defeated. He told the girl in whispers that it was time to go. That he was taking her home. She didn't want to go with him. Didn't want to leave the mother. She worried what would become of her; how she would get home. But the Wolfman was insistent and the girl tired. She followed him out to the car, climbed into the front seat next to him. His eyes were already heavy as he turned the key. The snow was thick upon the windshield and the Wolfman left the car to warm as he scraped the snow from it. But the snow was falling faster than he could clear it. He slid back into his seat, his beard and hair now white and wet, his fingers numbed.

All the way home the girl, normally quiet and thoughtful in her world which was removed from his, chatted incessantly, making note of every upcoming curb, every stop sign, every light, lest the Wolfman neglect to see them in his haze, through his half shut eyes. The girl's eyes, sober and wide, could guide them. Her heart was racing, the fear within causing it to pump harder, faster. The car slipped and slid on the icy gravel roads but somehow managed to avoid the blanketed cornfields, somehow managed to make it down the tree-lined driveway.

The Wolfman took the keys and stumbled toward the back door, forgetting the passenger left behind. The girl sat and stared out at the woods she knew so well, in no particular hurry to enter the house. She sat until the car grew cold and she could once again see her breath blown like smoke from her mouth. She forged a path of her own through the five or six inches that had accumulated on their lawn, feeling the wetness permeate her boots. A fresh slathering of mink oil would be needed in the morning.

It was Rufus, the red dog, who greeted her at the door. She let him slip past her and waited as he quickly relieved himself, then ran back into the house, into her arms. "I should have just stayed home with you tonight," the girl thought, as she nuzzled her face to his. They stepped over the Wolfman, unconscious where he had fallen there on the kitchen tile, and made their way up the stairs to bed. In the darkness of her bedroom, not bothering to turn on a light, the girl slipped into her red, flannel nightgown, the one that allowed her to pretend that she was Laura Ingalls and that Michael Landon was her Pa. She climbed under the many quilts that covered her bed. Rufus curled up next to her, under her loving fingers that combed through his fur in search of burs. She remembered, then, the tooth an arm's reach away. She grabbed it and placed it under her pillow before drifting off to sleep with the red dog.

In the morning, it would still be there.

"Sometimes," the mother would tell her when she had finally made it down the stairs in search of coffee at noon. "The Tooth Fairy can't make it. Sometimes she has prior engagements. Don't cry, honey. Try again tonight. I betcha she'll come tonight."

Pia Ehrhardt

Pia Ehrhardt lives in New Orleans with her husband and son. She's had pieces published in *Bridge Magazine*, *The Mississippi Review*, *Gingko Tree Review*, *Pindeldyboz*, *MonkeyBicycle*, the *Word Riot 2003 Anthology*, *LitPot*, and *Eleven Bulls*, and one of her stories was awarded a Fictionline prize. She's working on a novel called "In the Driveway." There's more of her at www.piaze.com

likes

Dark red lipstick. The smell and taste of coriander. Holding the Sunday New York Times in my lap and pretending there's a choice about which section I will read first.

dislikes

Entertainment Tonight. I mute it and still can't keep my eyes off of it. White noise. Narrow lanes of traffic.

Hail

Lydia and her new husband drove over to Destin to find a three-bedroom beach house, because her sister was going to vacation with them next month. For years they'd talked about taking a trip together — the mountains, a lake — but Lydia always had a change of heart.

It was easier to miss Bay than spend time with her. When Bay phoned, Lydia watched her number in the caller I.D. window and didn't pick up. She sent her nephew "sorry-I'm-late" birthday cards. She was shy around Bay's husband, Gerry. In high school he sat in front of her in typing class, and for awhile they hung around, smoked pot after class, before Bay and him got together.

Lydia's senior year, their parents had taken a beach vacation and left the two sisters at home. They said the girls were old enough to be trusted, put Lydia in charge, and rented a condo for the week.

The two sisters shared the car with no fight, and pooled money for beer and Lean Cuisines. Gerry brought pot over and they smoked in the kitchen. Bay put the lit joint in her mouth and shot-gunned her. Lydia inhaled the smoke, their lips as close as kissing.

Bay let Gerry fuck her for the first time. Lydia wanted every detail, so Bay explained how time got slow, how he spoke quietly. He was in no rush. It was like he was the girl. When he pushed inside her they were close as two people can get. Closer than you and me? Lydia had asked. Bay groaned, said it burned a little but was great.

Saturday night, Lydia fucked Gerry's friend on her mother's

side of the bed and made a rusty red mess. The guy skipped the kissing. He took her from behind, on his knees, and she could see them in her mother's dressing mirror. The sex looked mechanical and ugly. Lydia closed her eyes and listened to his legs slap against hers.

The stain guide said milk would get blood out, but it didn't work. After three washings in hot water Lydia could still see traces and she threw away the sheets.

Gerry came over Sunday night and fucked Bay in the living room. Lydia knelt on the landing to see. Their sex felt better than hers. She would rather watch them.

Lydia missed Bay. At family gatherings she dreaded seeing her sister and Gerry, all of that intimacy shoved in her face. Once Lydia saw their romance, she new it was the kind she would never have.

Lydia envied their dovetail life — high school — college — marriage — a kid — how they'd accumulated a private history of everyday junk, fights, sickness, sweetness that had nothing to do with her. Her first marriage had only lasted three years, and then she was single for the next ten. She and Ray met on an elevator during a power outage and married in the spring.

Lydia's two sons didn't understand why they never saw their cousin and she didn't have a reason they could hear, so now they were going to meet up at the beach.

The first house she and Ray looked at was pale yellow with a decent view of the water but it was made of cinderblocks and had tiny windows. The second house looked more promising — gray weathered cypress perched on ten-foot pilings with a wraparound deck. She left Ray and the realtor in the driveway to check out the beach access. She climbed the stairs. The door was cracked open so Lydia walked in but a woman was in the kitchen and they startled each other.

"I'm sorry," Lydia said. "I thought the house was vacant. Are you renting?"

"No. I'm with the cleaning service." She wore cut off khakis and a Florida Gators T-shirt, and looked concerned, like Lydia had walked in on something.

The kitchen table was covered with a red and white checked picnic cloth and there were half-eaten sandwiches on paper plates, sweating cans of Coke, a trail of Fritos.

"Well, this house isn't ready," Lydia said, like a hotel guest who'd come back from lunch expecting a clean room.

"The boy was killed this morning," the woman said. "The office must've made a mistake."

"Oh," Lydia said, taking a step back. "I'm sorry."

The woman shook Comet into the steel sink. "I guess since they're gone you can look around."

Big windows faced the Gulf. A section of the beach had been cordoned off with yellow tape and two jeeps and a patrol car were parked on the sand. Ray and the realtor were talking to an officer.

"What happened?"

"Shark attack," the woman said.

Lydia looked around the room. An open box of Nilla Wavers lay on the coffee table.

The woman washed the breakfast dishes. "The father just came back for their clothes." She dried a long serrated knife with a dishtowel and put it back in the drawer. "Only sand sharks come that close to shore. Something is wrong."

"Maybe the boy got between the mother and baby," Lydia said.

The woman shook her head. "They said he was only in up to his waist."

There wasn't a soul in the water in front of this house, but down the beach kids skimmed across the wet sand on body boards.

"Do you have children?" Lydia asked.

"A daughter."

Lydia walked around carefully. The closets were empty. She was afraid to touch anything. On the dresser was a colorful brochure for the new waterslide and theme park that had opened this summer.

Last year she'd brought her boys to the beach and they stayed at the Holiday Inn. Her sons had spotted the new park under construction — a skeleton of riggings and steps to nowhere. The family must have gone there because two wet Sea Escape towels were on the floor of the bathroom. In the kid's room the twin beds were unmade. Pokemon cards were on one, and *Teen Beat* magazine and a kit for making beaded bracelets were on the other. A brother and a sister. Now only a sister.

Lydia phoned Bay to see how she was.

"I was just getting ready to call you," Bay said, "You're going to kill me, but we have to cancel." She explained that a hail storm had come through the night before — walnut-sized hail — and torn up her roof and the neighbor's and dented Gerry's truck. "How in the hell does the sky make balls of ice?" she said. "Weird."

Lydia didn't know how hail formed, but it couldn't be bad enough to cancel their trip.

"The insurance adjustor is coming and then we have to schedule repairs," Bay said. "Gerry saved a few chunks as souvenirs and put them in the freezer."

Lydia wanted to tell her about the boy but Bay had to go, someone was at her door.

Lydia called her mother so she could talk to her sons. They were in the backyard bombing each other with water balloons.

"Are they okay?" she said.

"Sure," her mother said. "Are you?"

"Yeah, I just miss them."

"We're fine here. Just enjoy yourselves," she said, and hung up.

Lydia stared at the Gulf and looked for pink water. The tide pushed in.

The woman swept sand into a dustpan.

Lydia introduced herself. The woman's name was Marlise.

"I want to help." Lydia picked up the plates and cans and bags of snacks and placed them gently in her black plastic Hefty bag. It felt wrong to touch the family's things, like they were removing evidence from a crime scene.

Marlise had a small gold cross around her neck that swung forward when she leaned over.

"Do you pray?" Lydia asked.

"To Mary," Marlise said. While she dusted the furniture she spoke to Mary, asking for something over and over in words Lydia couldn't hear.

Lydia hadn't prayed since her sons were babies, when their high fevers would spike in the middle of the night. What would she say? This was the beach. A harmless place, the reason beach balls and Pro-Kadima and little plastic shovels and buckets existed. Kids didn't get killed tooling around in shallow water twenty yards from their parents. Parents worried about the undertow, not jaws.

Ray and the realtor were still talking to the officer, and a small crowd had formed. The wind was blowing hard out of the west. Ray had his hands in his pockets, his head down as he listened, and his shirt tails snapped behind him. Lydia knew he liked to stand with the wind in his face, that he ate spinach and artichoke dip with a spoon, and drank the spring water she left in her glass because it pained him to pour it down the drain. He fell asleep within minutes of closing his eyes. She loved the small, daily stuff in their new marriage, but she wanted everything — Ray's history — the events and memories that belonged to his first wife. And she wanted to unload hers — her lousy first marriage, all the dumb mistakes, park her heart in his garage. Where could she start?

The living room was bright and quiet. Outside, the sky was the most reckless blue with seagulls flying through it every which way.

Did they know a child was gone?

A dumb song popped into her head — *Oh, it's a jolly 'oliday with you Bert, a jolly, jolly 'oliday with you* — a silly pre-vacation song whispered to her sons, one last goof before bed. Lydia sang it just loud enough to change it from a thought. She wanted her family in one place.

She called Bay back and told her she had to come.

"You can't get a refund?" Bay said. "How ridiculous. This is an act of God."

"No, that isn't it," Lydia said, and tried to steady the shake in her voice. "I just need you."

"You do?" Bay said. She paused. "It's about time."

Bay was right. Lydia had quit her like a spurned lover when she started going with Gerry. Lydia didn't know how to love her sister and leave her alone with Gerry, how to quit wanting the parts of people she couldn't have, and graciously take what they offered.

"A boy was killed at the beach this morning by a shark."

"Oh," she said. "That's terrible."

"The house we're looking at right now is where he was staying. With his parents and sister."

Bay was quiet on her end of the phone. Lydia loved her for shutting up right then. For not paving over the sadness with something stupid like, *isn't that morbid?* "Okay," she said. "We'll work things out here and meet you in August."

"Maybe Mom and Dad can come, too," Lydia said.

"Is there room?" Bay asked.

"We can make it work," Lydia said.

"Anyone else?" Bay said.

"Some cousins?"

They would sit on the deck and watch the gulf, have drinks and talk and be thankful for any detail. And remember the family who had lost their boy. And not take their eyes off the kids. They would spend enough days together where a vacation stopped being so damn special and was just two sisters sharing a house with kids, the dogs, in a mess of toys and towels and snacks. One had a husband she'd loved since high school, and the other had a husband to love now.

Marlise sprayed Windex on the sliding glass doors. Lydia put the towels in the washer. She put the sister's bead kit and *Teen Beat* on the counter so they could be sent to the family, and she thumbed through the boy's Pokemon cards and chose one to keep in her wallet.

By the time Ray and the realtor came upstairs they had the

place clean. He looked so sad and worried as he reached for Lydia's hand. "Did you call the boys?" he said.

"They're fine," she said.

The realtor took her car keys out of her purse, awkward and ready to leave.

"We'll take it," Lydia said.

Max Ruback

Fiction published in *OysterBoy Review*, *New Orleans Review*, *Chattahoochee Review*, *Zing*, *Thrift*, *Crab Creek Review*, elsewhere. NonFiction in *The Writer*, *Turnrow*, *Main Street Rag*, and *Thought*. I am working on a collection of short fiction, titled, *Us Escaping Something*. Currently, I live in West Palm Beach, Florida. I can be reached at whereverhereis@aol.com.

likes

Finding great stories and essays and poetry in small lit mags, quiet days at my desk, possibility, Radiohead, Clem Snide, Grandaddy, Heather Nova, Pink Floyd, Neil Diamond, IFC and the New England Sports Network, a stranger buying me a drink, the underdog and the longshot, sometimes me, hope

dislikes

Those great stories and essays and poems in small lit mags having only a small readership, loud neighbors, bad dreams (If only I knew how to decipher them), MTVs portrayal of what they think music is, the cost of stamps for me to send stories out to mags, my own poor poor judgments, sometimes me, the late night thoughts of aging and death

Introduction To Still-Life

We stop drinking. We try to keep busy. We see a lot of movies. We learn backgammon. We sometimes play Scrabble, but we don't have the patience to keep our interests up. We can't really get together with friends, because our friends drink. We go for walks at dusk. We watch TV, have sex, fall asleep. We have less sex and watch more TV as days go by.

She signs up for a painting class one night a week at the high school, called, Introduction to Still-Life. I buy a remote control car. You build it yourself from a kit. I join a local club with other remote control car owners, men and boys. It's very competitive. We race on Saturdays. I get real into it. I think about the car when I'm at work. I fine-tune it every night, figuring out how to make it go faster. It's all about the speed. It's like love.

On Wednesday nights, she goes to class. She isn't enjoying herself early on. She says she's not very good. I try to cheer her up, tell her she just started, that she needs to give it time. I tell her it's obvious she has talent. She doesn't believe me, though. She wants so badly to be good at something. She won't show me her paintings, keeps them under a cloth, makes me promise I won't look.

I'm working on my car out in the porch. I'm adjusting the alignment.

You wanna play? she asks.

Play what?

Backgammon.

Let me finish this up. I'm almost done.

I win my first race. I want to celebrate with a beer, but I talk myself out of it, drive straight home with my trophy in the passenger seat, glancing at the passing bars.

Check this out, I say.

She' s watching TV, smoking. Cool, she says. Congratulations.

I lean down and kiss her on the cheek.

Where should I put it?

Wherever you want, she says, stabbing out the last of her cigarette. On top of the TV if you want.

You okay?

Fine, she says, lighting another. Just into the movie.

I want to sit next to her and kiss her, have sex, but I know she'll just tell me later. I go into the kitchen and clean the dirt off the car. I take it apart and get all the dirt out from the gears. You have to be like a surgeon. I wax the body. I stare at its beauty. I turn it on. The wheels spin.

Can you do that later, she says. I'm trying to watch this.

Sorry.

From the kitchen I watch her watching the movie. She's still so beautiful, I sometimes can't believe she loves me the way she does. I go over to sit next to her, just to be next to her.

We're playing backgammon. We drink green tea and eat crackers with discs of cheese and pepperoni on them.

Can I see one of your paintings? I ask.

I'm not ready to show you.

I want to see how you're doing.

I'll show you just one.

Thanks.

And only if you promise to tell me the truth. Don't just say something nice to make me feel good.

I won't.

I've seen her paintings already, even though she told me not to look at them.

She goes to the spare bedroom and brings back a painting. It's a bowl of fruit. It has an apple and a lemon and an orange inside the bowl.

You did that?

I'm still working on it, she says. I need to finish the background. Make it look more real.

That's really good, I say.

Stop, she says.

I'm not kidding. You got talent.

It's just an exercise, she says. No big deal. I need to finish the background.

It's a big deal. You should be proud of yourself.

Thanks, she says.

I'm proud of you.

She smiles, Thanks.

After awhile, I pay less attention to the car. It isn't as exciting as it once was. I get bored watching it go around and around the dirt track. Plus, some of the guys drink beer at the track and I keep giving in.

The guy at the hobby shop tries to get me into remote control planes, but I'm not that into it. It's the same as the cars, except in the air.

She hangs her paintings around the house. She's really getting good.

I want to have a drink. I want to just go to a bar and have some drinks and listen to a live band and be with the woman I love. I want to dance with her.

You wanna go out? I say. It's Saturday night. I don't want to go to the movies. I don't want to play backgammon. I want to get out and have some fun.

Where?

For a drink. We've been good, haven't we?

We go to Coasters. It's good to see our friends. They say they thought we disappeared. They say they thought we thought we were too good for them. They buy us the first round.

I sit next to her and put my hand on her thigh. We smile at each other. We kiss. We drink. We kiss we're so happy.

Andrew Bomback

Andrew Bomback, currently a research scientist at the New York State Psychiatric Institute, will begin an internal medicine residency next year. His stories have recently appeared or are forthcoming in *Pindeldyboz*, *Diagram*, *Elysian Fields Quarterly*, *New York Stories*, *Snow Monkey*, and *Crab Orchard Review*.

likes

flannel shirt weather, roughly 25% of Drag City's roster, lamb chops, the RFMH, Richard Yates, Larry David, the Brooklyn Brewery, the last line of "For Esme — with Love and Squalor" ("You take a really sleepy man, Esme, and he always stands a chance of again becoming a man with all his fac — with all his f-a-c-u-l-t-i-e-s intact."), the Knitting Factory, and "Tennessee," a song by the Silver Jews that must have been playing (on my stereo or in my head) when I started writing this story

dislikes

bunions (except the spelling, which is great), Oprah Winfrey, the Miami Dolphins, the direction Belle and Sebastian are headed in, McGriddles, the RIAA, Kevin Costner (the actor), Kevin Coster (the director), the staff at pretty much every Kinko's, and racism

20 Stories About My Dead Brother, Ollie

1.

I won't start with the obvious story, the one I'm sure you're interested in, because for starters that's not the way Ollie would have told stories about himself. And because your definition of obvious probably differs from mine. For me the obvious story to start with is the one that is my favorite, which is when I was six and starting first grade. That would make Ollie ten and a fifth-grader. My parents had decided to stop sitting in the chair next to my bed and waiting for me to fall asleep; they told me that I was big enough to fall asleep on my own. Ollie came into my room on the first night of this new arrangement to give me advice on how to fall asleep. "What I do is create this fantasy," he said, "where I'm like the world champion of wrestling, and I'm walking down the aisles to the ring, and everyone's cheering for me, and there are all these women kissing my muscles, and my arch enemy is waiting for me in the ring, and he's all scared because he knows I'm going to win. And I'm just so happy, you know, and confident. It's a great feeling." I never followed his advice. I didn't need to, to be honest. I just fell asleep back then. But sometimes now, when I'm having trouble falling asleep, I'll remember Ollie's pep talk, his fantasy, which doesn't help me fall asleep, but usually gives me enough of a laugh to stop worrying about not being able to fall asleep.

2.

A year earlier, when Ollie was in the fourth grade, he took a part in the school production of South Pacific. He was Sailor #3, I think, or maybe #4. A chorus part, nothing big, but Ollie was just entering his anti-social phase at this time, and my parents were relieved that he was still involved with something. There was a half-day of school — it must have been a Wednesday, because for some reason there were often half-days on Wednesdays — and when my mother picked me up from kindergarten she had Ollie's brown bag lunch on her lap. We parked the car and went inside the school, to the auditorium where after-school play rehearsal had not yet started. There were lots of kids sitting on stage, Indian-style, with their lunches on their laps. Lots of laughing, I remember, and lots of loud noise. Ollie was alone sitting in the audience, playing air-guitar or air-drums, something internal. My mother gave him his lunch and kissed him on the forehead. Then she told him he should sit on stage with the other children. Which he did. My mother and I stood in the auditorium for a few seconds, watching Ollie sit down next to a group of four or five boys. Then we left, and my mother took me to McDonald's for lunch. I went to the indoor playground after eating my lunch, while my mom stayed at our table reading a book. When I was tired from playing, I went back to our table and found my mother crying.

3.

In the summer of 1989, when I was fourteen, I took a job as a junior counselor at a local day camp. Ollie worked at the camp, too, as a chef. He said he enjoyed hanging out in the kitchen and listening to the radio. He said he enjoyed the company of the other kitchen workers more than the company of the camp's counselors. On an especially hot day, I went into the camp kitchen to sneak an extra pitcher of fruit punch for my group, and Ollie was sleeping in the kitchen's walk-in refrigerator. He was lying on his back, with just a bathing suit on. "Hey," I said, nudging him with my foot and then stepping over him to grab a pitcher. "Hey, are you alright?" He opened his eyes and smiled at me. He put his finger to his lips and smiled, as if we were sharing some top-secret joke.

4.

That same summer Ollie dated Inez, a Puerto Rican girl who was one of the camp's waitresses. She was a few years older than Ollie, a student at the community college just trying to make some extra money during the summer. Her family lived in Puerto Rico. That's really all I know about Inez. Their relationship was short, but afterwards Ollie often sat in our living room, watching a grainy videotape of a Puerto Rican beauty pageant in which Inez had competed when she was younger. He said she had given it to him, but I suspected that he had stolen it from her. Ollie memorized the lyrics to this Spanish song that Inez sang on the tape. A few years ago, when Ollie spent a weekend on my living room couch, I heard him singing that Spanish song in the shower.

5.

I might as well talk about that weekend a few years ago. I was twenty-three, in my second year of medical school, and Ollie was working at a restaurant in SoHo. He had been renting a basement room in Astoria from an elderly couple, and he showed up on a Saturday morning with a suitcase and a story about the plumbing backing up, the apartment being flooded. He stayed for the weekend and then took the train to my parents' house, where he ended up living for almost a year. At the end of that year, he was hospitalized for the second time. My father, recently, at a dinner where too much wine was served, told me that Ollie had deliberately flooded his Astoria apartment and had caused almost two thousand dollars worth of damage to the elderly couple's home. I didn't respond; my father took another sip of wine, put his arm around me, and said that he never really felt safe when Ollie was living with them for that year.

6.

The first time Ollie was hospitalized was during my Christmas break of freshman year. I came home after finals and was in a great mood. My parents met me at the train station and told me that Ollie had tried to kill himself. We spent Christmas Eve in the hospital with Ollie and the other patients on his floor. I bought him a bottle of cologne that he wasn't allowed to keep in his room because it contained alcohol. He told me that night that he liked the gift and hoped that I wouldn't take offense if he didn't use the cologne while he was in the hospital. "I mean, it's pretty sad that I'd have to go to the nurses station and let some orderly spray it on me, don't you think?" he asked me. I took that as a good sign — that he would be so tuned in to the sadness of his situation. I was young, and I was not ready to admit that my older brother was sick, so I was looking for anything to assure me that this was an aberration and that Ollie would never have to be in this kind of place again.

7.

I did meet Karen Winfield. I'm the only one in my family who met her. In fact, I'm the only one in my family who visited Ollie in Nashville. He called me up and told me that he had met this incredible woman and that he had asked her to marry him on their third date. I flew down to Nashville a week or so later for a long weekend. I had been meaning to visit Ollie anyway, and meeting Karen was a good excuse. She was very nice, much nicer and more normal than I expected from a woman that Ollie had decided to marry. I remember this trick Karen taught me about getting the smell of garlic off of your hands. This was after the three of us had cooked dinner, and she was standing by the kitchen sink rubbing a soup ladle all over her hands. She told me that the steel of the ladle absorbed the scent of garlic. "Isn't she great," Ollie said, and he put his arm around her.

8.

It was actually Ollie's psychiatrist's idea for him to leave New York. He thought Ollie might fare better in a new, less-pressured environment. Ollie chose Nashville because he'd always loved the Robert Altman movie and, as he said last Thanksgiving when he announced his plans, "I don't dislike country music." My parents bought him a used Saab to help with the move. I bought him some Waylon Jennings and Merle Haggard tapes for the trip. I don't know anything about country music, but the salesman at the record store said that those two were solid choices. I was aware then, and am still aware now, that we were in some way disowning Ollie. I'm sure Ollie forgave us, but, seriously, what kind of parting gifts are country music tapes? At least my parents gave him a car.

9.

I was a sophomore at Brown when Kurt Cobain killed himself. It was a pretty big moment; some classes — the ones that were taught by the younger, hipper professors — were even cancelled. That night Nirvana songs played from almost every stereo in my dormitory, it seemed. My friends and I sat in the courtyard outside the chemistry labs passing around joints and quoting as many Nirvana lyrics as we could, stunned in our newfound appreciation for Cobain's poetry. I went home around two in the morning, and there was a message on my answering machine from Ollie. "I just wanted to see how you were doing," he said. "I'm fucking depressed out of my head," he added after a few seconds of silence. I called him back, and he was probably drunk or high or maybe had decided to actually take some of the psychiatric medicines that he usually flushed down the toilet. But he sounded sleepy and peaceful, and for a second I worried that he might be in the middle of a suicide attempt. "I'm fine," he reassured me. "I'm going to get a tattoo on my back tomorrow, with the words 'I hate myself and want to die,' you know, from that song, and that's how I'm going to deal with this." I cannot recall seeing his bare back after this phone call, and I have no idea whether or not he actually went through with the tattoo. Although my guess is that it's something that would have made it into the newspapers when they found his body.

10.

Ollie went through a brief period in junior high school where he tried to be a rock star. He took guitar lessons in the back of a music store and learned enough chords to play a few Beatles songs at our church's talent show. My parents encouraged him to form a band with some friends, but he said that he wanted to be a solo act. The highlight of this period was the night when Ollie interrupted an episode of *Family Ties* to sing us his new, original song. He turned off the television and sang, "I get up, and nothing gets me down." He proceeded to sing an a cappella version of Van Halen's "Jump," and afterwards he stood with a big grin in front of me and my parents. "It's nice," my mother said. "Very catchy," my father added. "It's just a first draft," Ollie said. "I know it needs some work." "But it's a great start," my mother said. "Yeah," Ollie said, and he turned the television back on before leaving the room. "That's a real song," I said to my parents. "That's a song they play on the radio all the time." They didn't say anything, so I repeated myself. "We heard you the first time," my mother said.

11.
Ollie went to a small college in Connecticut that had a culinary arts program; it was a two-year school at which he spent three years, and my parents never took me when they drove the hour and a half to visit him. When he came home on school holidays, he prepared a special dinner for us, incorporating the new cuisines he had been studying. He would call the night before coming home with a list of ingredients that my mother would buy the next day. Sometimes he'd suggest a specific wine that my parents would drink with the meal.

12.
I took a semester abroad in Italy during my junior year of college. Ollie sent me a care package roughly one month into the semester: a pack of Topps baseball cards, three Stephen King novels, a box of granola bars, a Chapstick, four pairs of white socks, a 36-pack of condoms, a Kinks mix tape, and a five-dollar bill. His note ended with some brotherly words of encouragement: "Remember, wear condoms, but fuck like a champ!" The Kinks tape had the song "Death of a Clown" on sides one and two, which probably was an over-sight by Ollie, but I wouldn't put it past him to have been poking fun at himself. I listened to that song this morning — on a compact disc, as I lost

Ollie's mix tape when my backpack was stolen on a train in France — and found myself smiling instead of crying.

13.

"From the age of nine or ten until I went to college, I didn't have one friend," Ollie boasted to Karen during my visit to Nashville. "It's true, ask my brother. I was the quintessential loner, the original recluse." I tried to disagree, but I spent the four or five minutes it took me to drink a beer trying to remember a single friend. I could only come up with one figure, a small boy with an asthma inhaler who came over the house a few times. "No," Ollie said. "That kid, whose name was Brian Maloney by the way, was my assigned science project partner, so that doesn't count as a friend. We were working together." Karen looked at me, I raised my empty beer bottle in response, and Ollie put his arm around her. "I liked being alone," he said. "I was always very comfortable with my own company." Karen leaned her head on his shoulder, and I felt happy for Ollie. I wanted my parents to see him like this. "You know, kids are pretty astute, more aware than we probably give them credit for," he said. He gently slid his shoulder out from beneath Karen's head and reached for his beer. "They knew before anyone else how weird I was."

14.

When Ollie was seven, he opened up a new bottle of children's vitamins and ate all of its contents. We were alone in the kitchen. My mother was vacuuming in the living room, and she had left us with grilled cheese sandwiches for lunch. I watched him eat vitamin after vitamin; this is one of my earliest memories, the picture of Ollie's hands shoving vitamins into his mouth. Later that night, we went out to dinner at a Roy Rogers, and Ollie vomited after his first bite of fried chicken.

15.

Ollie picked me up from the airport in the used Saab that my parents had bought him. He alerted me to his bumper sticker — "I'll forgive

Jane Fonda when the Jews forgive Hitler" — and told me that it was the first thing he'd bought in the South. "So, I figured we'd drop your stuff off at my place, then grab some lunch before showing you around the city. And tonight, we'll meet up with Karen for dinner." "Sure," I said. "I'm excited to meet her." "She's excited to meet you, too." I remember thinking that this was such a normal conversation, the kind of thing any two brothers would say to each other. And although I was aware that there was something reckless and impulsive about Ollie asking a woman to marry him on their third date, I wanted to believe in him. That afternoon, as I soaked in the Nashville sites that Ollie included on his personal tour of the city, I hoped that this was the right place for him, the kind of city where dreams could come true at your own pace. Maybe Ollie's life would have a happy ending, I thought, like the ones in the country songs that were supposed to flow out of every Nashville bar. Admittedly, I hadn't really listened to much country music before the trip, and so I wasn't aware that most of the songs sung in Nashville turned out to be sad.

16.

Ollie was never a good athlete. Although it's a cliché (and one that I'm not certain is true), my guess is that Ollie was always the last one picked in gym class for any kind of team sport. He couldn't kick a ball very well, or throw one either. He wasn't fast or strong. He did possess one athletic talent: climbing. He could climb anything — fences, ropes, flagpoles — and he did so without the least bit of effort. I wonder if he ever talked about this with his psychiatrists, and whether or not they found something poignant in this skill, like the ability to escape or to raise himself above the world. I'm sure if a doctor said this, Ollie would have laughed at the suggestion. But I wonder. I wonder if he told anyone about that Saturday afternoon when I was seven and Ollie was eleven, and my mother took us both to Baskin Robbins for ice cream after my youth soccer game. I had scored a goal and my team had won, and Ollie told my mother that I deserved two scoops and sprinkles. Ollie had only played one season of youth soccer, and I would go on to play soccer through high school. After we ate our ice cream, Ollie pointed to the flagpole outside the post office that was in the same shopping center. He told my mother and me that he could climb it, and we said that we believed him. We stood and waited for him to run to the pole and climb to the top, but instead he walked to my mother's car and waited for her to open the door.

17.

Today's Nashville newspapers say that sometime yesterday morning Ollie shot Karen in her kitchen, and then went to her bathroom where he shot himself in her shower. Karen's neighbor said that first she heard yelling and then she heard two shots, roughly one minute apart. She called the police after the first shot; they found Ollie dead in the shower, and Karen died on the ambulance ride.

18.

Ollie played a trick on me when I was in elementary school. I think I was nine or ten, and E.S.P. was the hot topic of conversation that week among my friends for some forgotten reason — maybe it was the subject of a movie or a television show that we all liked, or something we read about in an assigned book. I asked Ollie if he believed in E.S.P., and he said that he believed it was a power we all possessed. "You just need to really concentrate, think really hard, and I bet you could read my mind." He told me to try, and I closed my eyes forcefully. When I opened them, I looked at Ollie's forehead and thought I saw a football stadium behind his skin. "You're thinking of a football stadium," I said. "Jesus Christ," he said. "I can't believe you just did that. Try again." I eagerly closed my eyes and opened them, this time seeing a television screen. I told him of my vision, and he told me he was thinking of the movies. I tried again, this time seeing a vision of Superman in Ollie's mind, which he confirmed. I was amazed, and I ran to the telephone to call my friend, Josh. As I was bragging about my powers over the telephone, I turned around and saw Ollie smiling at me. He started laughing and clapping his hands. He pulled his pants down and held his penis and said through his chuckles, "What am I thinking about now?"

19.

I have no idea what Ollie and Karen were yelling about yesterday morning. Maybe it was a "domestic struggle," as one of the Nashville newspapers says. I don't know what to tell you, but I suppose that you, like me, would like an explanation as to why he would have done something like this. The suicide is actually understandable — well, not understandable, because it's a terrible thing and he should have known how much his death is going to hurt my parents, and me — but at least I can go through some of the events in his life and pose a possible explanation for why he would give up on the world. I have no idea why he killed Karen. All of the newspaper articles mention Ollie's psychiatric history, as if this is the simple answer we're searching for; Ollie hallucinated, perhaps, and thought that Karen was the devil or, even better, a human with the ability to fly, and being a good Christian he had to undo such a blasphemous image. Ollie was crazy, I know, but that can't be the reason why he killed her. He was crazy, but he was not simple. I've turned my stereo on again and programmed it to play the Kinks' "Death of a Clown" on repeat. I want to learn all the words, and I want to believe that Ollie and Karen made some sort of pact. There was a coin flip, and Ollie's heads didn't come up, so he had to be the one who killed his lover before killing himself. The yelling was probably just for the neighbors' benefit.

20.

In my third year of medical school, I did a rotation on an adolescent psychiatry unit. I was assigned two patients: an anorexic girl and a schizophrenic boy. Although Ollie was neither anorexic nor schizophrenic — his numerous doctors never committed to one diagnosis, but he probably was bipolar with a personality disorder thrown in for good measure — I could not interview these two patients without hearing some of Ollie's voice in theirs. I suppose that's more of a story about me than it is about Ollie.